# The Reluctant Earl

## Joan Wolf

Untreed
Reads

*The Reluctant Earl*
By Joan Wolf

Copyright 2020 by Joan Wolf
Cover Copyright 2020 by Untreed Reads Publishing
Cover Design by Ginny Glass

ISBN-13: 978-1-94913-568-8

Published by Untreed Reads, LLC
506 Kansas Street, San Francisco, CA 94107
www.untreedreads.com

Also available in ebook.

Printed in the United States of America.

**Publisher's Note**

# PROLOGUE

"Carstairs, do you know where Lord Woodbridge is?" the Earl of Welbourne demanded in his usual chilly tone of voice. "He is supposed to be studying with his tutor, but apparently he's nowhere to be found."

Carstairs, Lord Welbourne's butler, knew quite well where his lordship's son was, but he maintained a blank face. The staff at Welbourne had grown adept over the years at protecting their young lord from his father. "I believe he went into the village to meet with a school friend who is visiting nearby, my lord. Shall I have him sent for?"

"No. I just happened to notice his tutor chatting with one of the maids—and that is *not* what I'm paying him for. Her either, for that matter."

The earl's aristocratic face was looking annoyed. It was the way he always looked when his eldest son was concerned.

The butler said, "Which maid was it, my lord? I shall speak to her."

"Do that, Carstairs. It was the young pretty one with the red hair."

"Kitty. I shall speak to her."

"See that you do."

"Will that be all, my lord?"

"Yes. Carry on Carstairs."

"Yes, my lord."

The tall, gray-haired butler moved silently out of the library. In the hallway he met Mrs. Willis, the housekeeper, who was looking worried. With one accord they stepped into a small salon on the far side of the hall and lowered their voices. "I heard he was looking for Lord Woodbridge," she said.

"Yes. I said he was in the village visiting with a school friend."

1

Her worn, pleasant face broke into a smile. "Very good. That should satisfy him." She glanced at the door. "What in the world made him ask for his young lordship? He never does that."

"He saw Mr. Allen talking to Kitty and was afraid his money was going to waste."

Mrs. Willis rolled her eyes.

Carstairs said, "I had better send a message to Mr. O'Rourke to make certain Lord Woodbridge comes home for dinner tonight."

She nodded, then lifted a hand to keep him from leaving. "Don't forget to include the excuse you gave his lordship. Lord Woodbridge will need to know what to say if he is asked."

"I'll do that."

Mrs. Willis said, disapproval clear in her north-country voice, "Not that Lord Woodbridge will be invited to eat in the dining room."

"He's better off in the school room," Carstairs said with a sigh. "Dinner with Lord and Lady Welbourne would be torture for the poor lad."

The housekeeper glanced toward the door, then said urgently, "Mr. Carstairs, Lord Welbourne must *never* find out how much time his young lordship spends with the O'Rourkes."

Carstairs produced a grim smile. "He won't if we can help it, Mrs. Willis."

The two of them had been in service at Welbourne Abbey since before Simon was born. They had been his fierce champions ever since his mother's death when he was five.

"I'll send Gregson down to the stud farm with a message," Mr. Carstairs said.

They both glanced once more toward the salon door. "I'll leave first," Mrs. Willis said. After he had given her enough time to get down the passageway, Carstairs followed.

*

When Claire and Simon arrived back at the stables from their daily ride, her father, Liam O'Rourke, met Simon with the news that he needed to go home.

Since Simon ate his dinner every night at Claire's house, this was an unusual statement. It was Claire who asked, "Why, Da?"

Liam looked at the beautiful blond boy who was standing next to his daughter. "Mr. Carstairs sent a message that your father was looking for you, boyo. Carstairs told the earl you were in the village meeting up with a school friend, so you'd best be showing yourself at the abbey this dinner time."

Simon handed his reins to a groom with a genial, "Thanks, Davey." Then, looking back to Liam, he said, "I'm amazed he even noticed I was gone."

"Mr. Carstairs didn't say why, but if he felt it was that important you return home, you had better go."

"You don't think your stepmother found out you were seeing Charlie?" Claire asked worriedly.

Simon shook his head. "Nanny would never peach on us." Like her husband, the earl's second wife disliked Simon—partly because the earl disliked him, but mostly because he, not her son, was Welbourne's heir.

"When you come back tomorrow, Maurice is ready," Liam said. "That abscess in his hoof has cleared."

Simon's young face lit with pleasure. "Good. How do you want me to start him?"

"Just hack him through the woods at first. We need to make certain he can go along quietly before we do anything else."

Liam O'Rourke had come to work for the Earl of Welbourne nine years ago, when an Irish horse he trained won the 2000 Guineas at Newmarket in stunning fashion. The earl had bought Fergus and hired Liam to come along as Head Trainer of his racing stable. Since then the Welbourne Stud Farm had known outstanding success. Liam had become the golden boy of English racing, with job offers pouring in every time one of his horses won a major race.

The earl paid Liam well, but there were other reasons why he didn't want to leave Welbourne. For one thing, Fergus, the grand horse that had brought him to England, was still at Welbourne, producing winners year after year. Then Elise, his wife, was very happy here. Elise was the daughter of a French comte, who had fled the revolution and ended up in Ireland, where Elise had met and married Liam. He adored his wife, and if she was happy, he was happy. And last, but certainly not least, he couldn't begin to imagine how he could part Claire from Simon. During the summer, when Simon was home from school, they were inseparable. She loved Simon like a brother, and Liam himself had come to love the boy like a son.

"Go along with you now," Liam said to both youngsters, and watched as the two of them walked up the long grassy aisle that ran between the mares' paddocks. At fifteen, Simon was six feet while Claire, at fourteen, came barely to his shoulder. As Liam started to turn away, he saw Simon bend his silver blond head toward his daughter. Claire slid her arm naturally through his and looked up to reply. Her dark brown hair, neatly tied at her nape, spilled down the back of her riding jacket.

For one unsettling second an alarm rang in Liam's brain. He frowned and looked more closely at the two figures walking up the hill that led to the cottage that was his home.

They looked the way they always did, walking side by side, absorbed in conversation. Claire's arm had returned to her side. Liam shook his head as if to clear it, then turned back to resume his day.

# CHAPTER ONE

It was the end of term, and seventeen-year-old Simon was packing his belongings when he heard a knock on his door. Simon had been elected Head Prefect for the last three years, which why was he had the luxury of a room to himself. "Come in," he called, and turned to see who his visitor might be.

Christopher Clarkson, a boy in Simon's year, opened the door. "Hullo, Kit," Simon said, straightening from the leather portmanteau he had been putting shirts into. "What can I do for you?"

The blond haired, baby-faced boy said hopefully, "I know you're not leaving until tomorrow, Woodbridge, and my father would quite like to meet you. Will you dine with us? He'll take us to the Turk's Head."

The Turk's Head had the best food in town, and Simon was tempted. He was also puzzled. "Why does your father want to meet *me*?"

Kit ducked his head and looked embarrassed. "I suppose I must talk about you a bit when I'm at home."

This surprised Simon even more. Once he was home with Claire, school completely vanished from his mind. But he could see Kit was embarrassed, so he said, "It sounds splendid. Tell your father thanks and I'd love to dine with you."

Kit came to fetch him at five so they could walk into town. The boys passed by the school's magnificent stone buildings, built in the time of Henry VIII, and all Simon felt at their sight was gladness he would never have to come back. They walked through the glorious stone gate on the west side of the quad and Simon suggested they shorten their walk by cutting across the meadows. Kit agreed and, as they trod across the damp grass, Simon inhaled the fresh scent of the earth and thought that tomorrow Liam would fetch him home and he would see Claire.

Kit's father was already sitting at a table along the wall when Simon and Kit arrived. The Clarksons were the sort of landed

5

gentry that Simon's father regarded with casual contempt. They had property, and they could call themselves gentlemen, but they did not have riches, rank, broad acres and ancient lineage. They could never aspire to the world of the Earl of Welbourne, and Simon knew his father would be annoyed if he learned his son was dining with them. This thought disturbed Simon not at all.

Kit's father stood and Kit said formally, "Lord Woodbridge, may I present my father, Henry Clarkson."

Simon smiled politely and held out his hand. Mr. Clarkson leaned over the table to shake it, and the smile that had formed on his lips died. The blood drained from his face and he clutched at the table as if he were going to fall.

Simon stepped around the table to grab the man by his upper arm. Kit grabbed his father's other arm and the two boys helped him to sit. Kit asked urgently, "What's wrong, Papa? You've gone awfully pale. Are you going to faint?"

Mr. Clarkson shook his head. "No, no. I'll be all right. Get me some water, Kit."

Simon signaled for a waiter and a glass of water was brought to the table. Mr. Clarkson picked it up in a shaking hand and drank. When he had finished, he put the glass down, visibly struggled to pull himself together, and said to Kit, "I'm all right, son. Just a bit of a shock, that's all."

"A shock? What shock?" Kit asked, looking around as if to locate the source.

Clarkson looked at Simon again and said in a strained voice, "Please sit down, Lord Woodbridge. Sit down, Kit. I'm fine. Please don't make a fuss."

Simon didn't think he looked fine, but he sat as requested, his worried eyes on Clarkson. He hoped the man's heart wasn't failing. How awful for Kit if his father died right in front of him!

The man shook his head, as if to clear it. To Simon's relief, some color came back into his face. He said in a stronger voice,

"You see, Lord Woodbridge, you very much resemble my younger brother. So much so that I was rather stunned, I'm afraid."

Simon, who was accustomed to people staring at him, was surprised by this particular comment. He picked up his napkin and tried to think of something to say in response to this extraordinary statement.

Kit spoke first. "Do you mean Uncle Tommy, Papa?"

"Yes." A little more color had returned to Clarkson's face. He said, "You must think me a strange sort of person, Lord Woodbridge, and I apologize. But the resemblance is remarkable. You see, my brother died some years ago, so for a moment I thought I was seeing his ghost." He tried to smile. "I do not normally do this sort of thing, I assure you."

Kit turned to Simon, "My uncle was a soldier. He was killed while on duty in Ireland."

Simon thought Liam and Claire would have little pity for an English soldier who was helping to garrison Ireland, but he murmured something sympathetic.

Mr. Clarkson's eyes were still fixed on Simon's face. "There is some difference. Tommy's eyes were gray, not blue, and he had a cleft in his chin. But otherwise the resemblance is very close."

The man's stare was making Simon uncomfortable, but he only said mildly, "I suppose these things happen sometimes." He glanced around the room and noticed a number of other students from the school in the dining room. Kit's father wasn't the only parent treating his son to a good dinner on this last day of term.

The server, a rotund man with a splendid mustache, arrived to take their orders. All three chose the Roast Beef and Yorkshire Pudding that was the inn's specialty. Mr. Clarkson ordered brandy for himself and a glass of wine for Kit and Simon.

Simon could see that Kit's father was still a bit shaken, and Kit was looking embarrassed. He cast around for something to say and came up with, "My father has an estate in Ireland. Near

Limerick, I believe. He used to go every year to hunt, but he hasn't been in a long time."

Clarkson said, "Tommy was posted at Limerick Castle when he was killed."

Simon thought it was more than time to change this subject, but couldn't think of any other topic to introduce.

Mr. Clarkson continued, "He was riding by himself along a country road when he was shot. He was in uniform, and his colonel told us an Irish rebel hiding in the woods probably picked him off. Tommy should never have been on that road by himself; the Irish resistance was quite active in the area. His colonel was very upset about it." He shook his head slowly. "He was only twenty-two years of age."

"How tragic," Simon murmured.

"Yes." Mr. Clarkson took a drink of brandy and set his glass down with a thump. "Enough of this sad talk, now. Kit tells me that you were undefeated in football this year."

"We were, Papa," Kit said with genuine enthusiasm. He began to talk about the last game they had played, and Simon joined in with relief. Soon the server appeared with their meals, and there was no more talk about this soldier who looked like him who had been shot to death in Ireland.

*

Liam arrived the following morning to pick Simon up, and he related his encounter with Mr. Clarkson as they drove home in one of the earl's curricles. The two horses hitched to the carriage were thoroughbreds Liam was teaching to drive, and they were a bit skittish as Liam maneuvered them out of the town.

One of the many things Simon admired about Liam was the way he took care of the horses that were not fast enough to race. He didn't just discard them, as so many other stables did. He taught them to do another job, and then he placed them with a good owner. Simon himself had helped to retrain a number of thoroughbreds as hunters.

"That is a very peculiar tale, boyo," Liam said when Simon had finished speaking.

"It bothered me," Simon admitted. "The man kept insisting I was the image of his brother."

"Your father never mentioned to me that he had property in Ireland."

"He never goes there. I think he might rent it out."

"Do you know where in Ireland this property is?"

"I believe it's near Limerick."

A farmer's vehicle was coming toward them and Liam steered the bays away from the center of the road, talking to them softly so they wouldn't spook. Once they were safely past, Liam said, "Limerick has been garrisoned by the English for almost a century, Simon. They took over after they massacred the Irish who were defending the town. I'm not that surprised an English soldier got picked off. We Irish have long memories."

As Simon knew, Liam had made a comfortable life for himself in England, but he never forgot the land of his birth.

An easy silence fell as they drove along the narrow lane. Simon looked from the wheat waving in the fields back to Liam's concentrated profile, and felt happy. He was going home. When finally they hit an open stretch of road Liam relaxed, glanced at Simon, and said, "I have a horse I think will make a grand hunter, Simon." "Which one is that?" Simon asked enthusiastically, and for the next five miles they discussed the horse and what specifically Simon would need to do to get him re-trained.

They were almost home when Simon brought up the other subject that was on his mind.

"When I was last at home, I had an odd encounter with Mr. Pitt, My father's solicitor."

"Oh?"

"I was waiting in front of the house for Roger to bring the carriage around to take me back to school—remember you couldn't do it—and Mr. Pitt came out of the house. His carriage was already waiting for him and I wished him a safe journey back to London. But he stopped, turned to look at me, and said the oddest thing: 'Lord Woodbridge, do you know about the money that will be coming to you when you turn eighteen?'"

Liam's eyebrows lifted. "There's money coming to you? *Did* you know about it?"

"No, I did not. Mr. Pitt told me that my mother's marriage settlement provided a trust for me when I turned eighteen. That he thought I should be aware of it. Then he walked out to his carriage and drove away."

Liam frowned. "Sure, and that's a peculiar way to hear about such a thing. Your father never mentioned this inheritance to you?"

"No. And it's made me think about a lot of things, Mr. O'Rourke. Do you know that I don't know anything at all about my mother's family? No one has ever told me if I have grandparents or aunts or uncles from her side. It's almost as if she was born in a vacuum."

Liam's frown deepened. "I always assumed they must be dead. You never mentioned them."

"I never mentioned them because I knew nothing about them."

"You never asked?"

"One doesn't ask my father things he doesn't want to speak about."

"True enough, boy," Liam said. "True enough. And you had the definite impression he didn't want to speak about your mother's relatives?"

"It's not just her relatives—he never speaks about her!" Simon heard the quiver in his own voice, and took a deep breath to calm himself.

Liam's soft Irish voice softened even more as he asked, "Do you have any memories of her, Simon? I know you were only five when she died, but sometimes memories from childhood linger."

Simon thought. "I remember snatches of moments," he said. "I remember she always smelled good. I remember how she would hug me—she'd hug me so tight sometimes that it hurt. But I liked being close to her. And I remember she was pretty."

"Do you know what she died of?"

"No."

Liam frowned thoughtfully. "Her relatives must have come to the funeral."

"There wasn't any funeral. My mother died when she was on a visit to Ireland, and she was buried there. I always thought that was why my father stopped going to Ireland, that it would remind him of her death."

One of the bays began to toss his head and Liam rubbed his back with the whip and spoke soothingly in Irish. The bay settled down and the pair continued to trot quietly along the road.

Liam said thoughtfully, "Ireland."

"Yes." Simon watched the horses' muscles moving smoothly under their dark bay backs. He said slowly, "Ireland seems to have come up rather frequently today, hasn't it?"

"I was after thinking the same thing."

They drove for a while in silence, each preoccupied with his own thoughts. Then Liam said, "Would you like me to find out what I can for you about your mother's family?"

Simon turned to him in relief. "Would you, Mr. O'Rourke?"

Liam nodded. "I'm thinking your father's solicitor might have suspected you didn't know about the inheritance and that's why he told you. His conscience was bothering him."

Simon slowly nodded. "Perhaps. He's a nice man, Mr. Pitt."

They drove for a few minutes in silence, Liam concentrating on the horses and Simon looking at the green fields on either side of the road.

Liam broke the silence. "What was your mother's maiden name?"

11

"It was Jarvis. At least I know that."

"There's a famous English banking family by the name of Jarvis. Do you think she might be related to them?"

"I don't know," Simon said fretfully. "I don't know anything! It makes me feel so stupid."

"You're not stupid, boy. Things have been purposefully kept from you. Let me look around a bit and see what I can find out."

Simon turned to look at Liam's profile, at the thin, aquiline nose and well-cut mouth Claire had inherited, and felt a rush of relief and gratitude. "I would appreciate that, Mr. O'Rourke."

Liam flicked his whip to keep one of the bays from leaning out and said, "Don't worry your head too much, Simon. Enjoy your summer. We'll get this sorted out."

"Thank you," Simon said, his gruff voice disguising his emotion. They spent the rest of the drive discussing the horses Liam had in training.

# CHAPTER TWO

The following day Simon stood beside the small river in Welbourne woods impatiently skipping stones. Claire and he had arranged to meet at their usual spot the previous afternoon, when Liam stopped at the cottage so Simon could say hello to Claire and her mother. As Claire and her parents were going to dine at the squire's, he had gone on to the abbey.

"I couldn't get out of it," Claire had whispered to him as Simon and her father were returning to the curricle. "Meet you tomorrow at the glen."

He had thought of nothing else all night. It would be bliss to be alone with her again. But mixed with the bliss was frustration. He was too young. *They* were too young. He was finished with school, thank God, but he suspected his father was going to pack him off to Oxford. All the Radleys had gone to Oxford. And all his father wanted was for Simon to be out from under his sight.

When were they going to be allowed to be together? And what might this inheritance mean to them?

He heard hoof beats and Claire came riding into the glen on Finbar, the little gray gelding her father had bought for her when she had outgrown her pony. She flung herself out of her saddle and ran into his arms. Their lips met in a long kiss.

It was so hard to lift his mouth away from her. The reality of Claire was always so much stronger than his dreams of her when he was gone.

She said, "I missed you so much."

His eyes devoured the face he loved. Her eyes were huge and brown, with remarkable long black lashes. Her shining mahogany colored hair was tied as usual at her nape and fell halfway down her back. She had clear olive skin, a narrow arched nose and lips that he could kiss forever. She and her father were the "black Irish," she had once told him – descended in part from the Spanish sailors that had been flung on the shores of southwest Ireland when the Armada had broken up in the sixteenth century.

"I missed you too," he returned.

They said that each time he came home.

She stepped a little away and looked him up and down. "Have you got taller?" she demanded.

"An inch, perhaps."

"Why do you keep growing and I don't?" she said, woeful as a child deprived of a treat.

It was an ongoing complaint and it made him smile to hear it again. He tipped her chin up with his forefinger. "You're perfect just the way you are." His eyes glinted with mischief. "Even if you are short."

She tilted her head. "I love it when you look like that."

"Like what?"

"Like a naughty little boy."

His amusement fled. "I was never a naughty little boy."

"I know." Her voice was very soft. "Kiss me again, Simon."

He lowered his head and she slid her arms around his waist, pressing herself against him, her head tipped back on her lovely slender neck. The kiss deepened and they clung to each other with rising fierceness. Simon felt the storm of hunger inside him, and he forced himself to put her away while he still was able to. She staggered a little, as she lost the support of his arms.

He was breathing as if he had been running. He looked at her and said, his voice unrecognizable even to himself, "You're so beautiful, Claire. I love you so much."

They had known each other since she had come from Ireland to Welbourne. He had been seven and she six, and they had become instant friends. Over the years, as they had grown, the innocent friendship had turned into something much more.

She whispered, "I love you so much, Simon."

His heart turned over as he looked at her. He could lose himself in her eyes, he thought, and took a step toward her, desperately wanting the feel of her soft breasts against him, her beautiful full mouth under his.

A horse squealed and they both jumped. First Claire, then Simon, turned to look at Finbar. His tail was swishing madly, and he was glaring at his hip.

"Something bit him," Claire said. She went to look at his flank, then stroked his neck and told him he was fine, to go back to his grass. After a few more tail swishes, one of which caught Claire on the arm, he did.

Simon watched her soothe the horse and forced himself to sit and lean his back against a tree. Claire dropped down next to him. Her shoulder touched his arm. He cleared his throat and remembered what he had wanted to tell her. "Do you recall that legacy I wrote you about?"

"Of course I remember it. Have you found out anything more?"

"My father still hasn't said a word, and I turn eighteen in a month. On our way home I told your father what Mr. Pitt said, and he's going to try to search for my mother's family. The trust was part of her marriage settlement, so he thinks they would be the ones to pay it out."

"Good. Da will find out for you." She gave him a dark look. "I wouldn't be surprised if your father tried to steal your inheritance, Simon. You need someone looking out for your interests."

"I don't think my father needs my inheritance—whatever it may be."

Claire's frown deepened to a scowl. "Your father...I wouldn't trust your father to give you a slice of bread if you were starving, Simon!"

He looked grim. "True."

She settled back against his arm. "Where *are* the earl and his witch of a wife?"

"At a house party in Yorkshire, I'm told."

"Where's Charlie?"

"He's home. His mother takes him to London when they go for the season, but not when she's only going to be away for a short time."

"That's nice. You'll get a chance to spend some time with him."

Simon pushed the hair off his forehead. "The poor little fellow. He's dying to ride a pony, but his mother won't let him." His voice turned indignant. "He's five years old, Claire! I was riding a pony when I was three."

"Be careful," she warned. "If she should find out..."

"Don't worry. Mrs. Adams likes me, and Charlie's a good'un. He won't talk."

Simon's horse decided that Finbar had a better patch of grass than he did and tried to edge the smaller horse away. Finbar snorted and dug in.

Simon jumped to his feet. "Admiral, stop that." He went over to the thoroughbred and walked him to the other side of the glen. Once there, Admiral obligingly dropped his head and began to graze once more.

Simon returned to Claire. "Your father said he has a new horse for me to work with."

"Yes. A really nice bay whose not quite fast enough. Da thinks he'd make a splendid hunter."

"Good." Simon loved working with the thoroughbreds that needed to be re-trained.

He sat next to her again. The byplay with the horses had steadied him, as had their conversation. He put his arm around her shoulders and when she snuggled up to him it was all right. He said, "Wouldn't it be wonderful if this inheritance was enough money for us to live on? We could get married then."

"Oh Simon, it would be magnificent!"

They sat in silence for a while, her head tucked into his shoulder. Then Simon said, "A very strange thing happened to me before I left school."

"What?"

He rested his chin on the top of her head and told her about his meeting with Mr. Clarkson. When he finished she sat up and looked at him. "That *is* peculiar. I shouldn't think too many people in the world look like you, Simon."

He shrugged. "Sometimes people see what they want to see. I probably don't look that much like his brother after all."

"Perhaps it was your coloring." She was quiet for a minute then added, "Still, it's weird."

"Yes. It made me uncomfortable."

She said reluctantly, "I have to get back. Mama has something she wants me to do."

He let her go and watched as she stood and brushed her skirt off. As he rose to his own feet, he said, "Are the poachers still active around here?"

"According to Geoffrey, they're worse. He thinks the squire is too soft on them." The squire, Geoffrey's father, was the local magistrate in charge of sentencing crimes such as poaching.

Simon paused in the act of straightening his jacket. "Geoffrey? Who is Geoffrey?"

"Charlotte's brother. I've mentioned him to you."

He knew about Charlotte. She was the squire's daughter and Claire's good friend. While Simon was at school, Claire had had been studying too—with Charlotte and Charlotte's governess. While he was learning Greek and Latin, she had been learning how to be a proper lady. It had served to pass the time for her while Simon was gone.

He said, "You never mentioned him to me."

She shrugged. "He finished school last year, so he's been around more."

"Do you like him?"

She shrugged again. "He's all right, I suppose. Not as nice as Charlotte."

Simon really wasn't worried about this Geoffrey fellow so he let the subject drop. Claire raised her hands to tighten the ribbon that bound her hair, and he looked at the stretch of her slim supple waist. He picked up her saddle and lifted it onto Finbar's back. She came over to his side and watched as he tightened the girth. He knew she was perfectly capable of saddling her own horse, but he liked doing it for her, and she was kind enough to let him.

He fastened the last buckle and looked down at her. "I am *not* going to Oxford this autumn. I meant what I said about our getting married if this inheritance is real."

"I don't want you to go to Oxford. I'm so tired of missing you all the time. I want us to be together. For always."

He looked down into her upturned eyes—those enormous, thick-lashed brown eyes that were the one thing about her that hadn't changed since she was six years old. He reached out and pulled her into his arms. "I love you so much, Claire. It's driving me mad, these long separations." His voice was ragged with emotion.

"I know," she returned, her voice muffled by his shirt. "Let's hope the inheritance is enough."

He nodded and forced himself to drop his arms and let her go. She put her foot in the stirrup and swung into the saddle. "Are you coming with me?"

"Yes. Just give me a moment and I'll saddle up."

The familiar act of saddling a horse calmed him and by the time they returned to the bridle path he was able to speak normally about other things.

# CHAPTER THREE

Liam and Thomas Weston, the local squire and Liam's friend, sat together in the public room of their favorite Newmarket tavern. They had spent the morning watching the Welbourne horses as they worked out on the Newmarket gallops. The room was quiet at this hour, and Liam and Squire Weston had taken their usual table under a print of horses running in the 1,000 Guineas Stakes. Liam sipped his beer and waited for his friend to stop enthusing about the horses he had just observed. When the squire finally ran out of accolades, Liam broached the topic that was most on his mind.

"I have a problem I'd like your help with, Weston."

"Of course," said the squire, wiping some foam from his upper lip and looking interested.

"Can you tell me what you know about Simon's mother? The boy is curious. He's never met any of her relatives."

Tom Weston's bushy brown brows lifted in surprise. "I know only what everyone in town knows. She was an heiress—a Jarvis, in fact. The ones who own the bank? She was the only daughter."

"Ah," Liam said slowly. The Jarvis Bank was one of the biggest banks in England. "So she did belong to that family."

"She did. Before Welbourne married he owed money all over the village—and all over London too, I'm sure. And old Jarvis wanted to marry his daughter into the nobility. You know how it is, O'Rourke. It didn't matter that Jarvis could buy and sell most of the nobles who looked down their long noses at him. The only way a Jarvis would ever be able to crack that closed circle was to marry into it. So that's what Jarvis did—he married his granddaughter to the Earl of Welbourne. The gossip around town was the earl got a huge amount of money in the marriage settlement. He paid off all his debts and started putting money into the stud farm. *You* know how much he paid for Fergus."

"I do that. Much good did being a countess do for Simon's mother, though. She died when he was only five, poor girl."

The squire signaled for another pint. "Aye, it was sad. Happened in Ireland. The earl has an estate there. He used to go over for the hunting. The hunting around here wasn't good enough for him. He wouldn't taint himself by riding out with *my* hounds. God forbid!" He received his third pint from the hands of the owner and took a long swallow.

Liam watched his friend enjoy his ale and contemplated how much he should tell him. The squire put his glass on the table, looked at Liam's still half-full first glass, and said slowly, "What's this all about? What's made Lord Woodbridge suddenly so curious?"

Tom Weston was a good man, Liam thought. He treated his family, his friends, his hounds and his horses with respect and affection. He was a man you could trust.

Liam told him about Simon's inheritance.

Weston was nonplussed. "The earl never said anything to his son about this?"

"He scarcely speaks to his son at all. Simon will be eighteen shortly, but he's still supposed to take his meals in the schoolroom. And the countess is just as nasty as the earl. Claire says she hates Simon because he was born first so her son can't inherit."

"Good God," the squire said. "That poor boy."

"He's had a rough go of it, and now it begins to seem as if the earl is looking to cheat him out of this inheritance."

"Why haven't the Jarvises stepped in?"

"I don't know, and I'd like to find out. Do you have any suggestions as to how I might go about it?"

The squire frowned down at his strong, square hands as they lay folded on the table in front of him. After a few moments he said, "Lord Woodbridge needs a solicitor to look into this. Even if he's eighteen he's still a child under the law, but if money has been misappropriated—especially Jarvis money!—I think a solicitor will be interested."

"Can you recommend a solicitor to me?"

The squire leaned back in his chair. "There's solicitors in Newmarket, but they specialize in horse law. I would recommend you go into Cambridge. There's a company there I have dealt with myself, Coke and Ambrose. They're very respectable; if they agree to look into this for Lord Woodbridge, they'll do a good job."

"I'll see if I can get an appointment," Liam said. "Thank you for the recommendation."

"This situation sounds like a rum thing to me. Good luck."

"We'll need it," Liam returned.

The squire glanced at the clock that hung over the tavern's stone fireplace. "I have a hearing to get to. Best be going."

Liam agreed, and the two men pushed back their chairs, walked to the weathered wooden door, and exited out into the misty summer morning.

\*

Two weeks later Liam and Simon were on the road to Cambridge under a heavy gray sky. Liam was driving his own horse and gig, with Simon in the seat beside him. Both horse and gig had been bought with the generous bonus money Liam always received from the earl when one of his horses won a major race.

Liam knew that what he was undertaking for Simon was in direct opposition to Liam's own interest. If the earl discovered what Liam was doing, he would most certainly lose his position. Which Liam did not want to happen. Liam knew he could get another job instantly should the earl dismiss him, but both he and Elise liked where they were. They had become part of the parish social circle, and they had made some good friends. Liam had even put his own money into adding on to the cottage. If they had to go to another place they would lose all of that.

But, as Liam had said to Elise when they were discussing their course of action, "The truth is, the earl's a bastard and if he's trying to screw Simon out of his inheritance, I'm going to stop him."

Elise had agreed.

\*

The drive from Newmarket to Cambridge wasn't overly long, and Liam and Simon reached the city before noon.

"We need to find Bridge Street," Liam said, as he slowed his mare to a walk.

Simon's head was swiveling back and forth, taking in the magnificent golden stone buildings on either side of them. "My father went to Oxford, but even Oxford couldn't be more beautiful than this," he marveled.

"It's grand," Liam agreed. "But keep a look out for Bridge Street will you?"

Simon looked at a signpost. "We're on Bridge Street, Mr. O'Rourke. I just saw a sign."

"Grand. Now look for 'Jesus Lane.' Coke and Ambrose have their office on that corner. It's a red brick building."

They found the building, they left the horses in the mews, and together, man and boy walked into the law office of Coke and Ambrose.

Their appointment was with Mr. Coke. The elderly secretary showed them into an impressive office lined by floor-to-ceiling bookcases filled with fat, leather-bound books. The man sitting behind the large desk was younger than Liam had expected, in his early forties perhaps. He rose when they came in and shook hands with his visitors.

"Shall I bring in tea, sir?" the elderly secretary inquired.

Mr. Coke looked inquiringly at his guests. "Not for me, thanks," Liam said.

"Nor me," Simon agreed.

Mr. Coke said, "No tea, John. I'll ring if I need you."

"Yes, sir, Mr. Coke." The secretary effaced himself quietly.

The man behind the desk looked from Liam to Simon and Liam watched the surprise on the solicitor's narrow, intelligent face as Coke took in Simon's extraordinary face. There was always that moment of astonishment for anyone who had never met

Simon before. Coke masked it well, however, and when he spoke it was with quiet dignity. "Lord Woodbridge, suppose you tell me why you have come to see me today."

Simon related his story, beginning with the comment from the earl's solicitor and including the information Liam had learned from the squire. His voice was level and his details were concise. Liam was proud of him.

When Simon had finished Coke looked into the air above their heads, his brows furrowed. Simon shot a quick glance at Liam and Liam gave a slight shrug.

Finally Mr. Coke said, "Such a bequest is highly unusual. It is possible to create a trust so that if the husband dies, part of the wife's money comes back to her. But to create a trust for the eldest son? Very unusual. In fact, I've never heard of it."

"But it can be done?" Liam asked.

"It must have been done if the earl's solicitor spoke to Lord Woodbridge about it. The question I would like to have answered is: can Lord Welbourne make a reasonable challenge in regard to the trust's legality? To answer that question, I should have to see the exact wording of the trust document. The wording of such a document would have to be very specific to ensure the earl could not touch it."

Simon asked, "Is it possible for you contact Mr. Pitt and ask to see the paperwork?"

"I can do that, but we have another issue here. You are underage, Lord Woodbridge. You cannot be my client."

"I will be eighteen in three weeks, Mr. Coke."

"Yes, but the age of majority in England is twenty-one, my lord."

"Can Mr. O'Rourke be your client then? He could act for me."

"Mr. O'Rourke has no legal status in regard to your lordship. He is not a relative and he has not been made your guardian by a court."

For the first time Simon sounded like the boy he was: "He's been more of a father to me than my own father ever was! He's the only one who cares what happens to me! There must be some way to make it legal for him to act for me."

"Lord Woodbridge," the solicitor said gently, "consider Mr. O'Rourke's position. He is an employee of your father. What do you think your father would do if he learned that Mr. O'Rourke was challenging his right to this inheritance?"

All of the color drained from Simon's face. "He'd dismiss him."

"Just so."

Simon turned to Liam, distress in his eyes. "I should never have brought you into this, Mr. O'Rourke. If you should lose your position...."

Liam held up his hand. "Hush, Simon. There is another way."

He turned back to the solicitor and the two men looked at each other. "I could contact the Jarvis family," Mr. Coke said.

"I'm thinking that's the path to take," Liam agreed. "They may not be pleased to learn about how Lord Woodbridge is being treated."

Mr. Coke nodded slowly. "I'll find out who represents the Jarvises and speak to him. Then we'll see what happens."

Liam got to his feet and held out his hand. The two men shook. Simon extended his hand as well. Then Liam said, "Would you mind waiting in the office for a minute, Simon? I have a small question of my own to ask Mr. Coke."

"Of course." Simon gave the solicitor his gravely beautiful smile and left the two men alone.

As soon as the door closed behind him, Coke said, "That is an amazing boy. Does he know how beautiful he is?"

Liam smiled crookedly. "He knows but he doesn't care. He's the least vain creature I've ever met."

Coke nodded, still looking at the door that had closed behind Simon. Then he turned to Liam. "What is it you wish to speak to me about, Mr. O'Rourke?"

"Your bill," Liam said bluntly. "Simon doesn't have two farthings to his name. If you will send your bill to me, I'll see it gets paid. If he asks me about it, I'll say you're willing to wait until he receives his inheritance. He'd be upset if he knew I was paying."

"Very well." Coke extended his hand one more time. "Lord Woodbridge is fortunate to have such a good friend in you, Mr. O'Rourke."

"He's a grand boy and I want to see justice done, that's all. Good day to you, sir."

Liam joined Simon in the front room, and they repaired to a local inn for sustenance before they set off for the drive home.

# CHAPTER FOUR

Mr. Coke acted with dispatch and within a few days he had sent a letter off to the firm of Elbury and Masterson, solicitors for the Jarvis family. The reply came from Mr. Richard Jarvis himself, the present head of The Jarvis Bank. He introduced himself as Lord Woodbridge's uncle and asked for an appointment with Coke, naming the day and time that would be most convenient for Jarvis. Mr. Coke replied that the appointment time indicated by Mr. Jarvis was acceptable, and he looked forward to meeting the banker on that date. Next, he sent an urgent letter to Liam requesting his presence at the meeting, since he was the person most familiar with Lord Woodbridge's situation.

Liam told Elise about the meeting, but said nothing to Claire or Simon. On the appointed day he hitched up one of his thoroughbreds and set off for Cambridge. He had given Claire his usual reason for making a trip—going to see a man about a horse—and he knew she would pass the excuse along to Simon.

Mr. Coke had arranged his office with several comfortable chairs and a table set for tea. Liam arrived first and Coke had a chance to fill him in on the Jarvis family background. Richard Jarvis was one of the most powerful men in the city. He was also one of the wealthiest. Simon's grandfather had died some fifteen years before, and Richard had taken over the bank leadership. There were two other brothers also involved with the bank, but Richard was the man at the top.

Coke and Liam had just settled into their chairs when Richard Jarvis was announced. Both men stood up again and turned toward the door. As Coke went to greet the newcomer, Liam looked him over. Jarvis was a tall, well-built man with thick gray hair and a nose like a knife. Lines scored the flesh between his nose and his mouth. Liam judged him to be in his fifties.

When Coke introduced Liam, Jarvis held out his hand. The banker had a firm grip and he looked directly into Liam's eyes as he shook. The impression Liam got from the face and the steady blue eyes was one of razor-sharp intelligence.

"Pleased to meet you, Mr. O'Rourke," Jarvis said.

"Thank you, Mr. Jarvis. It's an honor," Liam replied.

The three men sat and Coke offered tea.

"Not just now," Jarvis said. "First I want to hear about my nephew."

Both men turned expectantly to Liam, who began to relate the story of Simon's life. He wanted to be succinct, but he was determined to make Jarvis understand just how neglected Simon had been. He ended by saying, "The boy knows nothing of his mother's family. His father never speaks of them and Lord Woodbridge has just assumed he had no relatives on his mother's side. When he learned of this bequest, he asked me if I could do a bit of investigation for him. That is how we came to Mr. Coke."

There was silence from Richard Jarvis as he looked fixedly at the space just above Liam's head. His hands were gripping the arms of his chair so tightly that Liam noticed his knuckles had turned white from the pressure he was exerting. When Jarvis finally spoke there was a note of suppressed emotion in his voice.

"I am sure you must think badly of my family, Mr. O'Rourke, and I am grateful to you for your kindness to my nephew. Let me assure you that after my sister died, we tried very hard to have contact with Simon, but Welbourne wouldn't allow any of my family near the child. When Annabelle gave birth to Simon, Welbourne forced her to cut off all contact with us. After she died, he absolutely refused to allow us to see her son. My father tried to go to court to force the earl to let him have access to his grandchild, but..." here his face flushed and his eyes flashed, "Welbourne was an earl and the Jarvises were just middle-class bankers who had tried to jump up in the world by marrying one of their daughters into the nobility. It was made very clear to my father that Simon didn't belong to us; he was Welbourne's heir and he belonged to the earl. We were to keep away."

Jarvis shut his eyes for a moment and when he opened them again they were bright with unshed tears. "My father was livid. He actually drove to Welbourne and demanded entrance to the house." The lines in his face seemed to deepen. "Welbourne had his footmen forcibly take my father back to his carriage and he gave orders to the coachman to leave." Jarvis's mouth set in a grim line. "My father came home a broken man. He never got over losing Annabelle, and then, to lose her child as well. He took to his bed and died three months later. I never believed people could die of a broken heart, but my father surely did."

Liam said softly, "A tale of great sorrow, Mr. Jarvis."

"Yes, it is. It started when my father decided to marry my sister into the nobility. He was a brilliant man, my father, and incredibly successful, yet he was never accepted into the highest level of English society. In that closed little world, as I'm sure you have noticed," and here his eyes moved from Liam to Coke, both of them successful, middle class men, "in that world, virtues such as intelligence, moral fiber, education, talent, all of those splendid qualities, count for nothing without birth.

He paused, clearly trying to collect his temper. "Well...my father doted on Annabelle, his only daughter. She was a beautiful girl and he wanted her to have a title. She deserved a title, he thought. So poor little Annabelle, at the age of eighteen, was married to the Earl of Wellbourne, a man twelve years older than she."

"The marriage settlement must have been significant," Mr. Coke said drily.

"It was. Welbourne was deeply in debt and my father paid off all his creditors. My father also added enough money for the earl to bring his estates up to snuff so he would have a decent income for the rest of his life. The Earl of Welbourne did very well out of Annabelle."

Jarvis' voice was deeply bitter.

"I assume the bequest to Lord Woodbridge was included in the marriage settlement," Mr. Coke said.

"Yes. My father insisted upon it. Annabelle and Welbourne's eldest son was to receive the sum of one hundred thousand pounds, plus the interest it accrued while it was invested. I have invested it in the five percents, so it has increased in value quite nicely."

Liam stared in astonishment. *One hundred thousand pounds!* That was a fortune.

Jarvis was continuing, "Welbourne didn't like it, but my father had been so generous he couldn't protest. Compared to the money he was getting, it was a pittance."

Liam blinked at the thought of one hundred thousand pounds—plus interest—being called a pittance.

"Our solicitor drew up the paperwork for the trust and made sure it was worded in such a way that it could not be broken."

Coke said, "Eighteen is not the age of legal majority. Lord Woodbridge cannot legally have charge of his money until he turns twenty-one. Was there a trustee named to administer the money until he comes of age?"

"Yes. My father named me."

Thanks be to God it wasn't Welbourne, Liam thought.

"My position as trustee of the inheritance does not make me Simon's guardian, of course. His guardian will still be his father. But this inheritance gives me a legal reason to enter Simon's life, and I intend to take advantage of it."

"That would be grand," Liam said. "The boy needs someone to stand up to Lord Welbourne."

Jarvis sat for a moment in silence, his eyes on Liam. "Would you say that Welbourne was a more distant father than usual among the nobility, Mr. O'Rourke?"

Liam smiled wryly. "I'm not exactly an expert on the English nobility, Mr. Jarvis, but I would say the earl has gone out of his way to reject Simon. It's more than just the lack of time a busy father has for his offspring. It has always seemed to me a deliberate attempt to crush Simon's spirit. They don't even want him to see his little brother. He has to sneak time with Charlie when the earl and countess are gone." Liam shook his head. "I have always found it…diabolical. On the part of the earl—and his second wife, Simon's stepmother, as well."

"But why? Why not allow my family to visit my sister's son? Why isolate him as they have tried to do?"

"If I could answer that question, Mr. Jarvis, I would surely. But I don't know."

The three men sat in contemplative silence for a full minute. Then Richard Jarvis got to his feet, followed by the other men. He held out his hand to Liam and said, "You have been very kind to my nephew, Mr. O'Rourke. He is a lucky boy to have had you and your family in his life."

Liam smiled the light-up-the-world smile he had passed along to Claire. "In truth, Mr. Jarvis, Simon is as dear to me as my own son would be. He's a grand boy. None grander, in my opinion. I'm that happy he will know your family."

Richard Jarvis smiled back. It was impossible not to respond to that smile of Liam's. Then he turned to Coke and said, "I will handle all the bills attached to this case, Mr. Coke. Have them sent to my solicitor."

Liam thought about protesting, then he didn't. The Jarvises were well able to handle a few legal bills. He said, "I will tell Simon. He'll be that pleased."

After another round of handshakes the banker was gone, leaving Coke and Liam alone in the room. Coke turned to Liam and said, "I shouldn't worry about Lord Woodbridge's future any longer, Mr. O'Rourke. It's in good hands now."

"That it is," Liam said with great satisfaction. "That it is."

# CHAPTER FIVE

While Liam and Simon were meeting with Richard Jarvis in Cambridge, Claire was spending the morning with her friend Charlotte at Winsted, the Weston's house. Mrs. Weston was planning a picnic party for some of the young people of the neighborhood, and Charlotte had asked Claire if she would help with the invitations. The library at Winsted was an oak paneled room with a marble fireplace, glass-fronted bookcases, a big desk and an assortment of comfortable chairs. The two girls were sitting opposite each other at the desk when Geoffrey came into the room.

Claire's back was to the door, and Geoffrey looked at Charlotte, while holding a finger to his lips. He crossed the worn Persian carpet softly and put his hands over Claire's eyes.

"Guess who?" he demanded.

She had heard his step behind her and said calmly, "It must be some idiot who thinks it's amusing to try to scare people out of their wits."

He dropped his hands. "You knew it was me."

"You're not exactly light on your feet, Geoffrey." She smiled up at him. "I thought you were visiting a friend in Surrey."

"I was, but now I'm home." He pulled a chair closer to the desk and disposed himself comfortably. Geoffrey Weston was a good-looking young man with light brown hair and hazel eyes. He had his father's big frame but had not yet filled out to the size he would be in future. His hazel eyes swept over Claire, from the top of her smoothly drawn back hair to the soft black slippers on her feet. Claire always wore her old brown boots when she rode to the squire's house, but she kept a pair of indoor shoes in Charlotte's room, as well as a change of clothes in case she was caught in the rain.

"You're looking very well, Claire," he said.

Claire gave him an ironic look. "A compliment from Geoffrey," she said. "Amazing."

He grinned and looked at the writing paper on the desk. "Mother told me you were writing invitations for her. She's having some kind of a picnic?"

"Yes," Charlotte replied. "Just for a few of our friends. Mary and Frank Bingham, Louisa Merton, Harry Morse, Margaret Compton...." She looked at Claire. "Have I left anyone out?"

Claire said, "I thought I might ask Simon. He's home from school."

Geoffrey frowned. "The earl's son? He won't come to a picnic with the likes of us."

"He would if he was invited," Claire said.

Charlotte leaned forward. "Claire, if he comes he'll just put a damper on everyone's fun. We'll all be so conscious of how we talk and what we say.... It's not even worth having a picnic if that's going to happen."

"Simon will fit in just fine!" Claire said passionately. "He's not a snob!"

Geoffrey said, "I think Charlotte's right. We don't need some lordship condescending to us."

Claire put down her pen, pushed back her chair and stood up. "Fine. If Simon can't come then I'm not coming either."

She stalked to the door.

Geoffrey said, "Claire, don't be like that!"

She shot him a burning look over her shoulder and banged the door behind her. He looked at his sister in bewilderment. "What was that all about?"

"It's just... When it comes to Lord Woodbridge, Claire is totally blind, Geoff. Just because she's his friend she thinks that we can be his friends too. Mama says she has no understanding of English social distinctions. Lord Woodbridge may be *her* friend, but she's the granddaughter of a French comte. There's not a drop of noble blood in our family's veins, and the Welbournes have never done more than nod distantly to Mama and Papa after church."

Geoffrey said thoughtfully, "Perhaps it would be a good idea to invite him after all. Let Claire see his true stripes."

"It would not be a good idea," Charlotte said emphatically. "That family is so superior—Mama says that the vicar once asked Lady Welbourne to give out the prizes at the village school, and she looked at him as if he was asking her to wade into a pile of manure. In addition to all this, Geoffrey, I've seen Lord Woodbridge and he looks like some kind of Greek god. All the girls will be goggling over him."

Geoff blinked. "Are you funning me?"

"No."

Geoffrey frowned. "Just how friendly *is* Claire with this Greek god?"

"They're *very* good friends. I hardly see her when he's home. They're together all the time. He even lets her ride his horses."

Geoffrey's forehead smoothed. "That's it, then. Claire butters him up because he lets her ride his horses. Claire would butter up the devil if he had a good horse for her to ride."

"Geoffrey!" Charlotte said, shocked.

He grinned at her. "Only funning." He started toward the door. "It looks as if you're going to have to write all the invitations yourself, Charlotte."

"There aren't that many. I only asked Claire to help as a way of getting her to come over. When Simon is home it's as if I don't exist anymore."

"Are you jealous of him?" Geoffrey asked incredulously.

Charlotte bit her lip. "Claire is my best friend, Geoff. We have so much fun together. She even made taking lessons with Miss Harris fun. But...she likes Simon more than me." Her voice died to a whisper. "I suppose I am a little jealous."

It was a measure of his new maturity that he didn't tease her. Instead he tactfully changed the subject. "Are the parents invited to this picnic?"

"Of course."

"Mr. and Mrs. O'Rourke will make Claire come."

Charlotte brightened. "That's true. Mrs. O'Rourke and Mama are bosom bows. Claire will have to come."

"Preferably without the Greek god," Geoffrey said with a grin.

"I don't know," Charlotte said gloomily. "He's pretty friendly with Claire's mother and father as well." She waved a hand at her brother. "Now go away and let me finish writing these invitations."

Geoffrey went.

*

When Mrs. Weston learned that Claire had wanted to invite Lord Woodbridge to her picnic, and that Charlotte had refused, the squire's wife almost had heart palpitations. She scolded a sullen Charlotte for losing the chance of having a real lord visit Winsted, and she immediately sent a note to the O'Rourke cottage telling Claire that Lord Woodbridge would be very welcome to come to their simple little picnic.

Claire asked Simon that very afternoon and he said he would be delighted to go.

Five days later Liam, Elise, Claire and Simon walked out onto the back lawn of the squire's charming manor house and joined the party of young people and their parents already gathered there. Claire introduced Simon to the Westons and the squire shook his hand while Mrs. Weston bobbed a curtsey and said breathlessly, "We are so pleased you could join us Lord Woodbridge."

Simon smiled his attractive grave smile. "It was very kind of you to invite me. Thank you."

Mrs. Weston flushed. "It was our pleasure, my lord."

Elise distracted her friend by asking her a question about the food and Simon was able to turn back to Claire. The squire said jovially, "You two go on and join the youngsters. I believe the boys are getting up a game of bowls."

Claire introduced Simon to the group of younger people she had come to know over the years, and Simon assured them he would hate to be called Lord Woodbridge by Claire's friends, that his name was Simon. The bowls game started, and Simon soon disarmed his new acquaintances by playing well and enthusiastically. Simon knew how to get along with boys—his schoolmates had elected him prefect every year because they both liked and trusted him—and soon they were all calling him Simon with complete unselfconsciousness.

Claire played battledore and shuttlecock with the girls, then joined in with the boys at bowls. By the time they were called to eat the whole group were laughing and joking comfortably.

Geoffrey was the only one who did not seem pleased by Simon. The two young men circled each other cautiously during the entire afternoon, taking the other's measure. Claire, who was enjoying herself enormously, never noticed.

"A nice group," Simon commented as they drove together back to the O'Rourke's house.

She smiled up at him. "It was grand having you there."

"Then I'm glad I went."

When they reached the O'Rourke cottage, they found a groom waiting for them. "His lordship returned a few hours ago, Lord Woodbridge. He wants you to come directly to the abbey."

Claire felt Simon stiffen beside her. Liam, who had already jumped down from the gig he was driving, said, "He'll come right along, Johnny."

"Yes, sir." The groom smiled, showing a front tooth missing, then trotted back to the trap to wait. Liam and Simon looked at each other.

"He's heard from Jarvis' solicitor," Simon said.

"It looks like that, boyo. Do you want me to come with you?"

"No! I don't want your name involved in this, Mr. O'Rourke. I don't want to be the cause of you losing your position."

The three O'Rourke's were looking worriedly at Simon. His chin was up, his eyes were level, and he did not look young any more. "I can handle this on my own," he said.

"All right," Liam replied equably. "You better go right away."

"I will." Simon's crystal blue eyes met Claire's large, brown ones. "It will be all right," he said to her.

She smiled encouragingly. "Of course it will."

"I brought the trap for you, my lord," the groom said.

"I see that," Simon said. "Thank you, Johnnie."

Claire forced herself not to reach for him as he swung up into the flat front seat of the trap. Simon took up the reins, backed the horses so he could make an easy turn, and drove briskly down the path that would take him to the abbey. He did not look back.

# CHAPTER SIX

When Simon entered the abbey and asked for his father, a footman directed him to the library. He went along to the appointed room, his heart thumping but his lithe walk quiet on the marble tiles of the hallway. The library door was partially open and, as Simon raised his hand to push it open all the way, he heard his father's deep voice. Without a second thought, he stopped his motion and listened.

The countess' voice came next, shrill and furious. "Why did you never tell me that Woodbridge was getting this huge inheritance from the Jarvis family? One hundred thousand pounds! He gets one hundred thousand pounds, and you tell me you haven't enough money for me to go up to London this year? You're unbelievable. You went through all your first wife's money, and now you've gone through mine? You had better find a way to get your hands on that trust fund, James. And once you do, there will be no more gambling! Do I make myself clear?"

One hundred thousand pounds! Simon's heart leaped in his chest.

"I believe the old man tied it up pretty tightly, Helen." The earl's voice sounded grim.

"There has to be a way to break it. I never heard of such a thing. It's true my Papa inserted a clause in our marriage contract that some of his money would come back to me if you died first, but that's not an unusual arrangement. This arrangement is...well, it's ridiculous. And why did you never tell me about it?"

"I never told anyone. I had almost forgot it myself until Pitt received this peremptory letter from Jarvis' solicitor. Woodbridge will have to be informed. That banker fellow, Richard Jarvis, is named as the administrator of the trust. I'm going to tell him the trust can damn well pay for Woodbridge's Oxford education. I don't see why I should have to come up with the blunt when there's one hundred thousand pounds coming to him."

"There's a trustee for the money?"

"Until Woodbridge turns twenty-one."

The countess' voice rose. "Why weren't you named trustee? You're his father!"

The earl's laugh was bitter. "The old man didn't trust me. He wanted the marriage because I could give his daughter a title and his prospective grandson an earldom. He shelled out a huge amount of cash, Helen, to pull me out of River Tick, and he told me in no uncertain terms that I wouldn't get another penny." He paused and his voice hardened. "I've always had a suspicion the Jarvises were Jews originally."

"Jews!" The countess was aghast.

"Oh, they traipse off regularly to Church of England services, but I've always wondered about their origins. They came from somewhere in Austria, I believe. I doubt that Jarvis was their original name."

Simon stood like a statue in the hall listening to this disgusting conversation. His poor mother. How could her father have forced her to marry such a despicable man? It horrified him to think his father's blood ran in his own veins. He couldn't bear to listen to another word so he knocked once, pushed open the door and stepped into the room.

*

"There you are, Woodbridge."

"Good afternoon, Father. Good afternoon, Stepmother."

The countess stared at him, her light gray eyes cold as ice. She hated to be addressed as "stepmother," and Simon knew it.

*"I have some good news for you,"* the earl said. *He was* dressed for riding and looked impatient to be off. "It seems that your mother's father left some money for you to inherit when you turn eighteen."

"My mother's father?" Simon said, looking surprised. "Do you mean my grandfather?"

"Of course he means your grandfather," the countess snapped.

Simon's face was a mask of innocent politeness. "It's just that this is the first time I've heard my father say anything about my mother's family. I've sometimes wondered if perhaps she dropped from the sky."

"Watch your tongue, young man," the earl growled.

"And how much money is this inheritance, Father?" Simon inquired.

"I'm not certain. We shall have to let the solicitors work it out."

*Will he never stop lying?* Simon thought in despair.

The earl was continuing, "The money won't be yours to spend until you turn twenty-one, Woodbridge, so don't start thinking you're rich."

"Whose money is it to spend until then, my lord?"

"Your mother's eldest brother has been named your trustee. He will decide how much money to advance you until you are old enough to make your own decisions."

"I have an uncle too? This is certainly a surprise. How is it I have never met any member of my mother's family?" Simon was careful to keep his voice politely inquisitive, not confrontational.

Lady Welbourne said, "Your mother's family are bankers, Woodbridge. Merchants. Cits. Of course your father didn't want people like that coming into his home as if they were family."

"But they were family," Simon pointed out. "*My* family."

The countess was so furious she almost hissed. "You should thank your father for not allowing the taint of commerce to stain the purity of your Welbourne blood. And how do you repay him for his care of you? You spend all your time with that Irish brat! Her father is a *horse trainer*, for God's sake." The countess' eyes narrowed to slits of gray ice. "Why do you think I have kept you away from *my* son all these years? I did not wish Charles to be contaminated by such a one as you."

Simon stared at her for one, long, unbelieving second. "Do you really think that way?"

"Enough!" The earl shot his wife a hard look and turned to Simon. "I will inform you when Pitt hears more about this issue. That is all for now, Woodbridge."

Simon slowly removed his gaze from the countess' face. "Yes, my lord," he said, walked to the door and shut it firmly behind him.

*

"She actually said she wouldn't let you see Charlie because you'd *contaminate* him?" Claire asked in horrified disbelief.

"Her precise words."

They were on horseback, riding side by side along the well-kept bridle paths of Welbourne. Simon was riding Tim Tam, one of Liam's not-quite-fast-enough thoroughbreds. Liam liked the animal's personality and athleticism and thought he would make an exceptional hunter. Simon was trying to get him accustomed to going through the woods.

A rabbit hopped across the trail and Tim Tam shied and spun around. Claire, who was riding Finbar, waited as Simon got the frightened thoroughbred calmed down. As they proceeded with their walk, Simon said, "My father still thinks I'm going to Oxford next term. He even said he was going to make my uncle pay for university out of my trust fund. I wouldn't be surprised if he tried to dun my uncle for the money he's had to spend on keeping me all these years."

"Nothing that awful man does can surprise me." They rode for a few minutes in silence, then Claire said, "One hundred thousand pounds! I can hardly believe it, Simon. That's a fortune!"

He turned to look at her amazed face and grinned. "I know. But we have to remember I don't get the money until I turn twenty-one."

Her amazement turned to apprehension. "Are you going to have to go to Oxford after all?"

"No." For the first time in his life, he had power. He had money. He did not have to do what his father told him to. "I am not going to Oxford." His adamant voice reflected his resolve. "I am not leaving you again. I'll speak to my uncle and see what kind of allowance he will give me." He looked into the eyes he loved so deeply. "We'll work something out, Claire. We won't need a lot of money to live on, you and I." He paused, then spoke words that were torn from the deepest part of his heart. "I swore a vow to myself when I heard the amount of the inheritance." His eyes held hers in locked intensity. "I swore I would never be lonely again."

She reached her hand toward him.

A noise came from within the trees to their right as a squirrel jumped from branch to branch. Tim Tam's head shot up and he danced around, eyes dilated and nose snorting. He began to back into the woods. Finbar decided he'd join in the fun, and the two riders were occupied for a while in rubbing their mounts' necks, keeping them on the path, and murmuring reassuringly. When Finbar finally decided to stand quietly, Tim Tam followed suit; with some encouragement, both horses began to walk forward.

Claire picked up their conversation as if nothing had interrupted it. "It isn't as bad for me because I have my mother and father. But..." Her eyes were focused between Finbar's ears, and a tiny line dented her forehead. "It's peculiar Simon, but sometimes I feel as if a part of me is standing aside, watching me as I go about my day. It's as if the person who's talking to Charlotte, or helping Mama with the garden, isn't really me. It's some other girl who looks like me. The real me is just waiting for you to come home."

They stopped their horses and crystal blue eyes looked deeply into brown. Claire spoke first, a quiver in her voice. "Do you think they'll let us get married?"

He said calmly, "If they don't, we'll elope." He reached for her hand. "Will you elope with me?"

Her face cleared like magic. "Of course I will!"

He grinned, lifted her hand to his lips and kissed it hard.

She shivered.

They walked along in silence for a while. Then Claire asked, "Where does one elope to, Simon?"

"Scotland," he replied. "I looked it up in the library at school. The bans don't have to be called for a couple to be married in Scotland. We just have to get there."

"We can do that," she said confidently.

"We can if we plan carefully."

A bug buzzed around Tim Tam's ears and he shook his head in annoyance. Simon said, "Let's trot and get away from these insects."

Claire agreed and the two of them moved off, the horses, like the riders, in perfect harmony.

# CHAPTER SEVEN

Liam had a promising filly running in the Oaks at Epsom, and Lord Welbourne was so confident of victory that he invited a party of friends to join him at the track. The squire had planned to go to the race with Liam, but he canceled at the last minute. The earl's gamekeeper, John Evans, had caught three men poaching in the Welbourne woods, and the earl demanded they be brought up in front of the local magistrate (the squire) immediately.

"I'm getting fair sick of these poachers," the squire complained to Liam. "These three aren't even local lads—they're from Bury St. Edmund's. They shot at Evans when he and his men tried to arrest them. Someone could have been killed. This time these damn poachers are going to feel the full weight of the law. I'll have them transported, I will. Perhaps that will keep the city bullies away from us."

While the earl was away at the races, Richard Jarvis paid an unexpected visit to the abbey. Lady Welbourne had gone up to London for a few days, and Carstairs, usually so protective of Simon, confidently directed Jarvis to the stables. By now all the servants knew about Simon's inheritance and who Richard Jarvis was.

As his carriage made its way toward the abbey's lovely stone stable buildings, Jarvis wondered what to expect from this first meeting with his sister's son.

A boy with silver fair hair and a dark-haired girl were standing in front of the stable, both of them staring at a pony's lifted hoof, when Jarvis' carriage drew up. The youngsters straightened up, and two young faces turned toward Jarvis as he descended and walked toward them. For the first time ever Richard Jarvis beheld his nephew, and his eyes widened with shock. Annabelle had been a lovely girl, but this boy...if an archangel ever came to earth he couldn't be more beautiful than Simon.

Jarvis shook his head, as if to clear it, and said, "I am looking for Simon Radley, Lord Woodbridge."

The boy replied in a pleasant voice, "You have found him, sir. I am Simon Radley."

Jarvis looked into his sister's crystal blue eyes and felt a pain in his heart. How proud Annabelle would have been of this boy, he thought. He stopped a few feet from them and said, "How do you do, Simon. I am your uncle, Richard Jarvis."

All the color drained from Simon's face. The girl put her hand on his arm and closed it tightly, as if for support, and answered for him. "We have been looking forward to meeting you, sir. I am Claire O'Rourke. I believe you have met my father."

"I have indeed," he replied, looking down into a pair of enormous brown eyes. "I am pleased to meet you, Claire O'Rourke."

She had given the boy time to collect himself, and now Simon held out his hand. "How do you do, sir. Forgive my manners. You surprised me."

"I'm sure I did. I learned at the house your father isn't at home, which I think is extremely fortunate. I was hoping for the chance of meeting you alone. Is there somewhere we can talk?"

Simon shot Claire a quick look. Jarvis made a shrewd guess the boy didn't want to take him to the abbey and suggested, "Perhaps there is an office in the stables?"

Simon looked relieved. "Yes, of course there is." He spoke to the groom who was holding the pony, "I think it's an abscess, Toby. Soak the foot in a bucket of hot water and I'll look at it again later." Then, turning back to his uncle, "If you will follow us, sir, I'll show you the way."

Claire said, "Perhaps I should..."

Simon's voice was uncompromising, "I want you to come with us."

Jarvis noticed the way his nephew shortened his stride to accommodate the girl. He fell into step on Simon's other side and obligingly shortened his own steps as well.

The stable office was oak paneled and large. A book lay on the desk open to an illustration of a horse's skeleton. Simon gestured Jarvis to the big chair behind the desk and brought over two plain oak chairs for himself and Claire. They sat.

Jarvis spoke first. "May I ask you, Nephew, what has your father told you about my family?"

"My father has told me nothing," Simon replied. He had collected himself and his face was guarded.

"Nothing?"

"I never even knew my mother's family name."

Jarvis narrowed his eyes in anger. "That bastard," he said. Then, noticing Claire, he added hastily, "Excuse me, Miss O'Rourke."

"No excuse needed," Claire said. "I completely agree with your opinion."

Jarvis looked at her in amusement, then moved his eyes back to Simon. "You must have wondered about us, though."

"I did rather."

Jarvis said, "I'm afraid it is not a story that redounds to anyone's credit, Nephew." He then repeated the events he had first recounted to Coke and Liam. When he finished, Simon was looking stunned.

Claire, on the other hand, was vibrating with fury. "What is *wrong* with Lord Welbourne?" she demanded, brown eyes glittering in her flushed face. "What kind of man behaves like that to his own son? I wish one of those poachers Mr. Weston is so concerned about would put a bullet through the earl instead of a deer! Then we'd be rid of him and could be happy!"

Simon looked at her and, very faintly, shook his head. His young face was set and grim. He turned back to Jarvis and said, "My father has never liked me."

Guilt, an emotion he was not accustomed to, stirred in Jarvis' conscience. "I am sorry, Simon. None of us had any idea of the situation here at Welbourne. We always assumed your father wanted to keep his wife's filthy merchant family away from his noble heir. In the end we decided—*I* decided—it would not be to your advantage for us to disrupt your life. I first learned of Welbourne's behavior toward you when Mr. Coke contacted my solicitor and I met with him and with Mr. O'Rourke." His mouth set in a hard line. "I have failed you, and I failed Annabelle as well. She would have expected me to look after her son."

Claire said fiercely, "My mother and father have been looking after Simon very well!"

A faint smile deepened the corners of Simon's eyes as he turned to her. "That they have, Claire."

"I am glad to hear that," Jarvis said sincerely.

Claire folded her hands in her lap and held Jarvis' eyes with a fearless intensity. She said, "Since you have deigned to visit Simon at last, Mr. Jarvis, perhaps you will be good enough to explain his inheritance to us."

She said *us* with perfect naturalness. Jarvis' eyes moved to his nephew. Those painfully familiar eyes were as steady and intense as Claire's. Annabelle's son said, "I understand it is a large amount of money. Can you explain to us how the money will come to me? Are there any conditions I must meet?"

There was that "us" again. "Of course I will explain it, Simon," he said, using his nephew's name for the first time. "It's quite simple, really. My father set aside one hundred thousand pounds of his fortune in a designated account to be invested for you until you turned eighteen. I invested it in the five percents, so your inheritance has grown quite nicely over the years."

There was the sound of a sharply indrawn breath. Jarvis didn't know if it had come from Simon or Claire. He paused a moment, then went on. "To be perfectly frank, the reason for the trust was that my father had little confidence in your father's financial sense. I don't know if you are aware of this, but when your parents married, your father was deeply in debt. My father, your grandfather, bailed him out of the debt as part of the marriage settlement. To be fair to Welbourne, part of the debt had been passed down to him from his ancestors, but my father had little use for the aristocratic class and the way they spend money. He didn't want to see his good money go to pay for gambling debts and bad investments."

Two pairs of eyes, blue and brown, were fixed on his face with breathless attention. He cleared his throat and went on. "The trust was added to the marriage settlement to make certain that you, the future earl, would have money available to you when you came of age. My father hoped the sound financial blood of the Jarvises would prevail in your nature and make you a more reliable investment than your father."

A small silence fell as the youngsters digested what they had just heard. Then Claire said, "What seems strange to me, Mr. Jarvis, is that if your father had so little faith in Lord Welbourne, why would he allow his daughter to marry him?"

As he looked into that lovely, innocent face, Jarvis felt suddenly very weary. He said, "My father arranged the marriage because he wanted his daughter to be a countess. It's as simple, and as foolish, as that."

Claire looked even more bewildered. "But your father was tremendously rich. Why should he care about a title?"

"Money doesn't buy entrance into the upper levels of society, Miss O'Rourke. The doors that were firmly closed to Miss Jarvis would open wide for the Countess of Welbourne. It was important to my father to have that kind of acceptance."

Simon and Claire exchanged wondering looks.

"I'd rather have the money," Claire said.

"So would I," Simon agreed.

"Ah," Jarvis said, looking at the beautiful boy in front of him. "You are so accustomed to being an earl's son you don't realize how differently you would be treated if you were simply Mr. Radley, a banker."

Simon didn't look convinced. He leaned a little forward and asked, "Can you explain to me how this money will be transferred to me? I know that the age of majority in England is twenty-one. Does that mean I won't have control of the money until I am of legal age?"

"My father named me as trustee, and until you reach the age of twenty-one I will administer the trust funds for you."

"Administer them how?" Simon's expression was intent.

Jarvis smiled. "I have no intention of being a pinch purse, lad. I will give you a quarterly allowance and expect you to live within it. If you encounter any unusual expenses, you may come to me. But I tell you now, Nephew, I won't pay any gambling debts."

Simon's quiet, "I don't gamble," clashed with Claire's indignant, "Simon never gambles!"

"I am pleased to hear that," Jarvis said.

"What if...what if I should need money for something personal?"

"You may come to me. I am a reasonable man, Simon, and I understand your father has kept you poor. Well, it's not a bad thing to be poor. You appreciate money more when you do have it."

"Yes, sir." Simon said.

"Can you take away Simon's allowance if he does something you don't approve of?" Claire asked.

Jarvis had the distinct feeling that there was something behind all these questions, but he couldn't quite see what it might be. "I could," he answered. "But I'm certain the issue won't arise."

Silence from the two youngsters. Their faces gave away nothing of what they might be thinking.

Jarvis said pleasantly, "I understand you have completed school. Are you planning to go to university?"

"No," Simon said.

Jarvis raised a surprised graying eyebrow. "No? What do you plan to do with yourself, then?"

The two youngsters looked at each other, then back to him. More silence.

Jarvis decided to try another subject. "What subject did you like most in school?"

"Maths. I liked maths. I did very well in them, sir."

"Did you indeed?" Jarvis added humorously, "Perhaps you would like to come and work in our bank."

There was a startled silence and the two youngsters exchanged another unreadable look. "Perhaps I could," the boy said slowly. "Would you pay me a salary?"

Jarvis was nonplused. The future Earl of Welbourne could not possibly work in a bank. He managed to say, "Please, Simon, won't you call me *Uncle Richard*?"

"Uncle Richard," Simon repeated obediently.

Jarvis decided this was not the time to list all the reasons why it would be impossible for Simon to work in a bank. Instead he smiled and stood. "We'll see how this all works out, eh?" His voice was genial. "In just a few weeks' time you will turn eighteen; we can discuss your future then."

Simon and Claire jumped to their feet as well. "Yes, sir," Simon said. "I shall be looking forward to that."

Simon held out his hand and Jarvis shook it. Then Claire held out hers, and her handshake was as firm as Simon's. They both were suddenly radiant. Jarvis wished he knew what was going on here, but contented himself with the knowledge that the man who had the purse strings had the control, and he was that man.

Simon and Clare stood side by side and watched until the carriage was out of sight. Then Simon turned to her, a brilliant smile on his face. "I'm going to have an allowance. I may even have a job. We can get married, Claire! We can get married!"

# CHAPTER EIGHT

The Welbourne filly won the Oaks. Liam was beaming as he came into the cottage and found Elise having tea in the parlor with two of her friends. She took one look at his face and clapped her hands.

"You won!"

"We did that. She's not a big girl but she ran like a champion. I expect to get some grand foals out of her."

The two ladies added their congratulations. The squire's wife said, "My husband will be devastated he couldn't make it. He's so very grumpy about these poachers."

"We'll run her again," Liam said. "At Ascot, perhaps. He'll have a chance to watch her then."

The two women tactfully made their goodbyes to Elise and left Liam alone with his wife. She smiled up at her tall husband and thought how little he had changed since she had fallen in love with him so many years ago. She had loved him almost from the first moment she saw him, and had married him against the wishes of her father, the exiled Comte de Sevigny. She had not ever regretted her choice.

He bent his head and kissed her. "I missed you," he said.

"I missed you too."

He kissed her again, and she put her arms around his waist and leaned into him. *I am a happy woman,* she thought. *How good God was to me when he sent Liam into my life.*

"Where is Claire?" he asked.

"Simon took Tim Tam for a ride and Claire went with him."

"Good. I think I may have a buyer for the horse, someone I met at Epsom. I'll have Simon school him over a few fences to make certain he'll jump."

"I'm sure he will."

"I'm starving," he said.

Their housemaid had come into the room to clear away the tea things and Elise said, "Leave the seed cake, Nancy. And can you bring a fresh pot of tea for Mr. O'Rourke?"

"Of course, Mrs. O'Rourke." The girl put the seed cake back on the table and picked up the almost empty teapot instead.

Elise said, "Come, sit down and tell me about the race."

Liam took a seat on the sofa beside his wife and described his week-long stay in Epsom, all the while eating the rest of the seed cake and drinking fresh tea. He had just finished the last drop when the parlor door opened and Simon and Claire came in. Nancy brought in some more teacakes and another pot, and Liam once more recounted the story of his filly's victory in the Oaks. Then he told Simon about the possible buyer and the two of them discussed how they would try Tim Tam over fences.

While the men were talking, Elise stood and drew her daughter aside. Claire still rode astride when she went out with Simon, and Elise still sewed divided skirts for her. Claire owned a sidesaddle, and she rode in it when she went into the village or to pay calls on friends. She had protested at first, but when she saw how upset Elise would be if she persisted in riding astride outside the estate, she had given in.

Elise looked now at her daughter and repressed a sigh. Occasionally she reminded Liam that Claire was his daughter, not his son, but she felt guilty that she had never given him a son and so usually she let them do as they pleased. She treasured the closeness of her happy family and wanted nothing to disturb it. But Claire was almost seventeen and Elise knew it was her duty as a mother to look toward her daughter's future.

"Ada Weston was here earlier," Elise said to Claire. We were talking about the first assembly room ball of the summer. I have agreed to be one of the patronesses this year since you're old enough to attend."

"A ball?" Claire said in bewilderment.

"Yes, a ball." Elise smiled. "You're almost seventeen, the appropriate age for a girl's first dance. You and Charlotte can go together. Mrs. Weston saw to it that you both learned to dance, and Geoffrey and his friends will be there to dance with you. You'll have a wonderful time."

Claire glanced toward Simon, who was still talking to Liam, then looked back at her mother. "When is this dance?"

"In two weeks." Elise did not want Simon to attend and tried to think of a way she could prevent Claire from inviting him. "You're not a child any longer, my love. You're a young lady. You should be looking to the future, to your own husband, your own children, your own life. You cannot go on forever being your father's daughter and Simon's sister. We all have to grow up sometime, and your time has come." Elise smiled and smoothed a finger along her daughter's high cheekbone. "You've turned into a beautiful girl, ma petite. Mrs. Weston tells me Geoffrey is quite taken with you."

Claire didn't know what part of her mother's speech surprised her more, the fact that Elise thought the relationship between her daughter and Simon was that of brother and sister, or her comment about Geoffrey.

"Why are you looking so surprised?" Elise asked gently.

Claire picked the lesser to two evils. "*Geoffrey?*"

Elise smiled encouragingly. "Wouldn't it be lovely if you married Geoffrey? He's a fine young man from an excellent family. And, just think, you would be living close to us."

"I have never thought about Geoffrey that way," Claire said flatly.

"Well maybe you should start."

Liam finished his conversation with Simon and crossed the room to ask her a question. Elise judged she had said enough to plant an idea in her daughter's mind.

*

The earl came back from Epsom brimming with good humor. He had bet heavily on his filly, and she had won for him. His Jockey Club friends were openly envious of his amazing string of winners. All in all, it had been a splendid week of racing. He had even won some money on other horses.

The only shadow on the earl's horizon was, as usual, his eldest son. Woodbridge was going to inherit one hundred thousand pounds. Every time the earl thought of that large sum of money he wanted to throw something. He could make far better use of it than Woodbridge. Over the years the earl had won money on his own horses, but his bets on horses that were not his own had been disastrous. He had also lost a great deal of money at Watier's. Honor demanded that those debts be paid immediately, which had put him in the position of having to borrow from a moneylender. The sad fact was, he had gone through both Annabelle's and Helen's fortunes, and here he was, in debt again. And now one hundred thousand pounds, which the earl desperately needed, would go to Woodbridge!

Well, he would pack the brat off to Oxford until he turned twenty-one. After that…. The earl scowled and poured himself a large brandy, which he drank in one gulp. What would happen to the money if Woodbridge died, he wondered? As his father, *he* would be Woodbridge's heir. Did that mean the money would come to him?

The earl poured himself another large brandy, sat on the velvet sofa in front of the fire, stared into the flames, and thought.

# CHAPTER NINE

The earl and countess did not celebrate Simon's eighteenth birthday. The only event that marked the day as more significant than his previous birthdays was that his uncle, Richard Jarvis, paid a visit to Welbourne. Jarvis' purpose was to discuss the trust money and tell Simon what he had decided would be an appropriate allowance for the next three years.

The earl and countess had removed themselves from the distasteful proceedings by visiting friends in Yorkshire, leaving five-year-old Charlie at home with his nurse. Simon and Charlie were kicking a ball around the side lawn of the abbey when Jarvis pulled up in his carriage. The two boys went to greet the newcomer.

Jarvis smiled at the picture they made. Charlie was almost as fair-haired as Simon, but his eyes were a darker blue and his features less finely cut. He was an attractive youngster, however, and was happy to meet Simon's tall, broad shouldered uncle.

"Me and Simon kicked the ball," he confided. "I kicked it all the way over there." He pointed to a lofty oak spreading its welcome shade across the lawn. "Simon says I'm strong for my age."

Jarvis smiled down at the eager little boy. "I'm sure you are. Does Simon kick the ball too?"

"Simon kicks really far. He can kick it all the way into those trees!" Charlie pointed to an attractive group of beeches that were shading a curved stone bench from the warm sunshine.

Simon picked up his little brother and put him on his shoulders. "Come along, old man. It's time you had your luncheon, and I need to talk with my uncle."

Charlie beamed down from his elevated position. "Are you my uncle too?"

"No, lad. You and Simon had different mothers."

Charlie's face sobered and he said anxiously, "You won't tell my mama that I was playing with Simon, will you?"

Jarvis threw Simon a startled glance. Simon turned away, refusing to meet his eyes. "Of course he won't say anything," he said to Charlie. Then, over his shoulder to Jarvis, "We can go inside. My father isn't home."

At the front door Simon turned Charlie over to one of the footmen to be returned to the nursery, then he led Jarvis into a small reception room that opened off the hall. Jarvis had been inside the abbey for his sister's wedding, so he knew how magnificent the rest of the house was. He himself preferred comfort to splendor, although he was a collector of English landscapes and had a number of fine paintings hanging in his own country home.

There were several yellow silk-covered chairs lining the reception room and an elegant desk that looked to Jarvis as if it was French. A tall gilt mirror hung over the desk and long yellow silk drapes hung at the single tall window.

"Is this all right?" Simon asked, looking at the folder of papers in his uncle's hand. "We could go to the library...."

He clearly felt uncomfortable about taking his uncle to the library, and Jarvis gave him a reassuring smile. "This is fine, lad. Just fine. I wanted to speak to you about what plans I have made and then I'd like to hear your thoughts."

Simon nodded gravely. A slant of sunlight from the window caught his hair, making it look as if there was a silver halo around his head. Again Jarvis felt a stab of sorrow and guilt at the way Simon had been neglected.

Jarvis began, "You have been at school for most of your growing up years, am I correct?"

"Yes, Uncle. I started when I was six and finished a few months ago. I know my father wants me to go to Oxford, but that's only because he wants me out of his way. I don't want to do any more school."

He had told Jarvis that once before. "Are you certain, lad? Boys of your class almost always go to Oxford or Cambridge. I thought it was expected of you."

"I'm not going."

Simon's face was set and his eyes were shuttered. It wasn't right for a young boy to look like that, Jarvis thought. He nodded slowly. "All right. But if you're not going to continue with your schooling, what plans do you have for your future?"

The boy was so still he scarcely seemed to breathe. When he didn't answer right away, Jarvis went on, "Do you wish to live in London? If that is your plan, I must tell you that I think eighteen is far too young..."

Simon lifted a hand to stop him. "No, Uncle. I don't want to live in London."

Thank the Lord for that, Jarvis thought. He looked once more at that closed face. What could the boy be thinking to make him look like that? He tried again, "Do you want to remain here at Welbourne? Learn about the estate, about what you will need to know when you become the earl? If so, I think that is..."

Simon was shaking his head. Emphatically. "I can't live here at Welbourne. I told you that my father doesn't like me, but the real truth is, he hates me. I don't know what I've done to make him feel that way, but there it is. He hates me." The boy pressed his lips together and shook his head, clearly unable to continue.

To give him time, Jarvis picked up the folder he had laid on the French desk and took a paper out. How dreadful to be made to feel hated by your own father. Welbourne had a lot to answer for, Jarvis thought grimly.

"You get along well with your brother," he said. "He seems to be a nice little boy."

"He is. We have fun together."

"Why did he ask me not to tell your stepmother you were playing with him?"

"She hates me too. She acts as if I'm going to contaminate Charlie by being near him. I would never hurt Charlie. I love him."

Something was deeply wrong with the picture Simon was painting. This was more than neglect...this sounded out-and-out ugly. Jarvis dropped his eyes to the folder he was holding, drew a deep breath, and returned his gaze to Simon. He spoke softly, "Do you remember your mother at all?"

The boy's eyelids lowered and he shook his head. "Not very much. I was only five when she died."

"She was only twenty-two. My family was shattered when we got the news. Annabelle was the youngest and the only girl. My father never got over her loss."

"She died in Ireland. She was all alone; my father hadn't gone with her." Something in his voice made Jarvis' throat tighten.

"I know, son. By the time Welbourne informed us, she was already in the ground. My father was livid, but there was nothing he could do. He didn't even have the comfort of being able to visit her grave. His health wouldn't allow him to make such an exhausting trip."

"I've never seen her grave either." The simple words went straight to Jarvis' heart. He cursed himself again for not having made more of an effort to know this nephew. "Perhaps you and I can go together some day," he said.

Simon met his eyes. "I'd like that."

"Good."

The boy managed a faint smile. "Please don't feel sorry for me, Uncle Richard. Claire and her family have always been there for me. They are my real family; my father and stepmother are just a nuisance I have to put up with."

"I'm very glad to hear that. The O'Rourke's seem to be splendid people."

"They are." Simon's face lit with enthusiasm. "Mr. O'Rourke lets Claire and me help with the racehorses. Right now I'm training one of the colts, who didn't do well on the track, to be a hunter. Mr. O'Rourke always makes sure the horses that don't work out as racehorses learn to do something else. He wants them to go to good homes, and my job is to see to it that they're ready for a new life. And Claire helps break the young horses. She has hands like silk and she's light on their backs. Mr. O'Rourke says she's the best person he has for that kind of work."

"I see."

He didn't really. Was O'Rourke mad, having these two youngsters work with racehorses? He could get them killed.

He asked, "Does your father know you're...er...training horses for Mr. O'Rourke?"

Simon made a dismissive gesture. "He's never asked me what I do and I've never told him."

"Do you plan to continue to work for Mr. O'Rourke now that you've left school? Because I doubt your father will permit that."

A flash of alarm showed on Simon's face. "I thought *you* were my legal guardian now."

"No, I'm only the trustee of your inheritance; your father is still your legal guardian, and he will be until you turn twenty-one. My only responsibility is to administer your money. What you do with yourself, well that is your father's provenance."

"So you're saying he still has the ultimate power over me," Simon said flatly.

"To some degree, yes. But you will have the right to use your money as you choose."

The boy nodded slowly. His light, crystalline blue eyes, so like his mother's, fixed themselves on Jarvis. "Have you decided how much of an allowance you are going to give me?"

"A hundred pounds a quarter. That will be taken out of the money your inheritance is earning from investment; it won't touch the principal."

Jarvis had given a great deal of thought to this amount. It was a large amount of money to put into the hands of so young a boy.

He had finally decided to begin generously and watch what happened. If Simon showed any tendencies toward dangerous extravagance, he could always lower the amount.

Simon's smile was sudden and dazzling. "Thank you, Uncle Richard! I appreciate your generosity."

"I have here a check on the trust account. Any English bank will honor it."

He held out the check. Simon took it, glanced quickly to check the sum, then stood and held out his hand. "Thank you, Uncle Richard. Thank you with all my heart."

Jarvis took the slim, strong hand into his and felt tears sting behind his eyes. Thank God for that trust, he thought. If it were not for his father's insistence on its inclusion, he would never have found Annabelle's son. *I won't fail you, Simon,* he vowed silently to himself. *I promise I will never fail you again."*

# CHAPTER TEN

The day after Simon's birthday Claire reluctantly drove into Newmarket with her mother. Elise had been insistent upon the necessity of adding to Claire's wardrobe now that she was a young lady of "marriageable age."

Claire had been shocked when her mother mentioned a possible marriage with Geoffrey. Even more shocking had been her mother's apparent belief that Claire regarded Simon as her brother. It was true that they had kept their love a secret from her parents, but...her brother? Had it never crossed her mother's mind that Claire might want to marry Simon?

Now, as they drove along in the pleasant summer sunshine, Elise chatted on about dances, and picnics, and a drive to visit some ancient church, all of which would make "nice outings" for the young people of the parish. She never once mentioned that Simon might like to partake of these "nice outings" as well.

What would her mother say if Claire told her that Simon and she wanted to get married? This was the thought in Claire's mind as her horse trotted smartly along the country road. They were almost in Newmarket before Claire plucked up the courage to say, "What about Simon, Mama? You haven't mentioned him. Don't you think he would enjoy these...er...nice outings?"

When her mother didn't immediately respond, Claire glanced at her. Elise had a small frown on her face.

"Mama?"

"Oh Claire, my beloved daughter. I know how much you care for Simon. And you know your father and I care for him too. But you're not a child anymore, *ma chere*. You are a young lady, and it's time to be looking around for a good husband. I know what will happen if Simon attends these gatherings. You'll be so focused on making sure he is enjoying himself that you'll ignore all the boys who qualify as suitable husbands for you."

"Like Geoffrey Weston?" Claire forced the name though stiff lips.

"Geoffrey is a fine young man, and his mother tells me he is interested in you. I would like you to give him a chance, Claire. If you don't wish to marry him, fine. There are other boys who find you attractive. But you will never get married if you insist upon introducing Simon into every opportunity you have!"

Claire said carefully, "Perhaps Simon is also looking for a wife."

"Simon will not be looking for a wife at a local assembly dance, I promise you that. One day he will be the Earl of Welbourne. His family will expect him to contract a suitable alliance with a girl of his own class."

"What if he doesn't want to marry 'a girl of his own class'?"

"I doubt that Simon will be given the choice, ma petite."

"Simon's mother wasn't an aristocrat."

"No, but she was a great heiress. None of the local girls can boast that attraction."

"But suppose Simon fell in love with one of those girls?"

"If he doesn't have the opportunity to meet the local girls, he can't fall in love with one of them," Elise said practically. "And even if he did, ma petite, he would not be allowed to marry her. An Earl of Welbourne does not marry the daughter of a solicitor, or a country vicar, or even a squire."

Considering what Elise had just said, Claire knew it would be disastrous to broach the subject of her own marriage to Simon. Fortunately, the red brick buildings of Newmarket were just coming into sight, and she was able to ask, "Where do you want to go, Mama? The High Street?"

"We should begin there certainly," Elise replied. "Ada Weston told me Barton's had some new gowns that were quite lovely."

"All right." Obediently, Claire steered her horse toward the road that would take them into Newmarket's most popular shopping area.

*

When they finally returned to the cottage, Claire immediately changed into her divided skirt. "Da was going to set up a course for Simon to try out Tim Tam's jumping skill and I want to watch," she told Elise, who was in the kitchen with Nancy conferring about dinner. Elise smiled serenely at her daughter and waved her off.

Liam had set up a course in one of the large paddocks and, when Claire arrived, Simon was just taking the big bay over the last fence. Claire watched approvingly as the horse tucked his knees up tight and cleared the fence with half a foot to spare.

She waited while Simon and Liam talked, both of them patting the thoroughbred, who was blowing through his nose and looking pleased with himself. Finally Liam signaled to a groom to take Tim Tam and cool him out while he and Simon fell into step and headed toward where Claire waited.

Simon's face was alive with pleasure. "He's a natural over the jumps," he said as soon as he was within speaking distance of Claire. "Did you get a chance to see him?"

"Only the last jump," she replied. "I thought he looked wonderful. He had his legs tucked tight and that's not something you can teach. Either they do it or they don't."

"I had an interested buyer in Epsom, but I believe I might offer him to Weston instead," Liam said. "He wants a new hunter for Geoffrey and Tim Tam would be a good match."

"What kind of a rider is Geoffrey?" Simon asked.

"Quite decent. I've hunted with him and he has a quiet seat and he's not too busy with his hands. He lets his horse do what needs to be done."

Simon nodded, satisfied.

"I won't charge Weston what I would have charged the Epsom man, but the earl is wealthy enough to withstand a small cut in price."

Liam always referred to the horses as his horses, but of course their real owner was the Earl of Welbourne.

Simon said to Claire, "I thought I'd work a bit with Desi. I wanted to put Charlie up on her, but she hasn't been ridden in so long I want to make sure she's not going to buck him off."

"I'll go with you," Claire said immediately.

A groom came running up to Liam and said something in a lowered voice. "I'll come right away," Liam said. He glanced toward Claire. "Make sure the both of you are home in time for dinner."

"Of course, Da," Claire replied.

The two of them returned to the front paddock, where Simon had set the horse he was driving to graze. They caught Bartholomew and brought him to where the farm trap was standing. Simon harnessed the black horse to the cart and they both climbed into the front seat. Simon picked up the reins and started off toward the hill path that would take them to Welbourne. When they were out of sight of the barns and paddocks of the stud farm, Claire asked, "Did your uncle come to see you this morning?"

"He did." He shot her a grin. "He's giving me a huge allowance, Claire. A hundred pounds a quarter!"

"That's wonderful." She bit her lip. "We need to talk, Simon."

He frowned. "Is something wrong."

"I'm afraid there is."

He stopped Bartholomew and turned to look at her. "What is it?"

She swallowed. "Can we go somewhere besides the road?"

He looked around. Thick trees grew to the left of the track and the river rushed along in its deep gorge on their right. "There's that old fishing hut down the road," he said.

She nodded and pinched her lips together to keep them from trembling.

The fishing hut was a tired-looking wooden shed on the bank of the river, with a steep path that led down from the road. There was just enough room for the trap to turn around at the bottom to come back up.

Simon got out and led Bartholomew down the path, with Claire in the front seat holding the reins. He tied the horse loosely, Claire jumped down, and they both went into the hut.

The smell of fish assaulted their nostrils the minute they opened the sagging door.

"Whew!" Simon said, fanning his hand up and down in front of his nose.

"This is ghastly," Claire agreed. "Let's just sit outside. Nobody will come by."

They found a mossy spot that was shaded by the hut. When they were seated, with their backs braced against the shed, Claire recounted her earlier conversation with Elise. "My mother was certain that your family would not allow us to marry, and Mama knows the ways of the nobility. I'm afraid that your father might pack you off to Oxford and not let us see each other again."

Tears filled her eyes.

Simon grasped her hand. "Don't cry, Claire. Please don't cry. We won't be separated. I won't let it happen. I promise you—*I won't let it happen.*"

"But you're not twenty-one, Simon. Your father still has control over you. And look how much he hated the Jarvises, just because they were bankers. He'll hate me even more—the daughter of his horse trainer. And Da will lose his job!"

She gave up trying not to cry and let the tears stream down her face. He pulled her into his arms and she sobbed helplessly against his shoulder. He said, his voice sounding desperate, "Don't cry, please don't cry, my love. We won't give them a chance to stop us. We'll elope."

At those words she lifted her tear-streaked face. "Could we really do that?"

"Yes, we can. I have in my possession a check for a hundred pounds that my uncle said I could redeem at any English bank. A hundred pounds should get us to Scotland."

She struggled to control her emotion and think. "But—even if we did get married—I don't know, Simon. I don't trust your father. He'll do something bad. I know he will."

"I agree with you about my father, and I've been thinking we should rely on my Uncle Richard. I'm certain he'll help us. He loved my mother, and I think he feels guilty for neglecting me for so many years. He's a powerful man, Claire."

This was true; she had heard her parents talking about the Jarvis Bank. She tried to wipe her tears away with her fingers as she asked, "Where in Scotland should we go? How far away is it?"

"I'll find out. We can do this, Claire. We have to. If we don't, we'll have to wait until I'm twenty-one."

"No! I don't want to wait that long to be with you!"

"Neither do I." He ran his thumbs along the wet cheekbones of her upturned face. "I love you so much," he whispered. She flung her arms around his neck and he kissed her. He kissed her as if he wanted to devour her, and she responded with a rush of passion she had not known existed. His body came over hers and she slid to the ground, her whole life narrowing only to this, to the fire of Simon's lips on hers, the strength of his young body pressing her to the ground.

Then, suddenly, he wasn't there. Shocked, bereft, she sat up, pushing her loosened hair away from her face. He was standing by the river, his back to her. She could hear how hard he was breathing.

"Simon?" she said in a wavering voice.

"I'm sorry Claire." He turned his head and managed a crooked grin. "That's another reason we had better get married soon."

She nodded dumbly, rose to her feet and went to put her arms around his waist and her cheek against his back. In a fierce voice she said, "We belong to each other, and no one and nothing can keep us apart!"

Finally he turned. He looked down into her eyes and said gravely, "We'll elope to Scotland and get married. I'll find out all about it and that's what we'll do."

She smiled through her tear stained face. "Good."

Tired of waiting, Bartholomew whinnied. Simon tore his eyes away from her and said, "I'm coming, you impatient beast. I'm coming."

He led the horse back up to the road, then took the reins from Claire to drive back toward Welbourne.

# CHAPTER ELEVEN

Simon asked Claire to tell her parents he wouldn't be available the following day as he was spending it with Charlie. His actual plan was to drive into Cambridge to do research.

The sky was overcast on the morning Simon left for Cambridge. He wanted to make certain that he had not misunderstood the Scottish marriage laws, so he went first to the university law library. He read the pages dealing with marriage in Scotland four or five times, and was relieved to find he had been correct. He and Claire were old enough to be married in Scotland.

The next item on his agenda was to check the schedule of the Royal Mail, which traveled daily from London to Edinburgh. A groom at the stable where he had left Bartholomew told him the mail always changed horses at the George, a coaching inn just outside Cambridge. Simon then rode out to the George, a large, busy establishment on the Great North Road. After consulting the route maps, he bought two tickets to Carlisle. They were expensive, but the mail was the fastest public transportation available; a private carriage was beyond his means.

It began to rain as he rode back to Welbourne, and by the time he reached the abbey he was soaked through. Before he went into the house, however, he rode into the woods, dismounted, and put his hand into the hollow of the big oak tree that shaded their glen. Inside he found a note.

Mama would like you to come to dinner. I hope you're home in time so I don't have to make up an excuse. Also—warning—she wants you to help clean out the attic tomorrow. It's for one of the vicar's charities. Better say yes and then we can talk.

Simon went back to the abbey, changed his clothes and rode over to the O'Rourke's for dinner.

\*

Elise had determined to see what she could find in the attic to donate to charity. Newmarket and its surrounding area had pockets of extreme poverty, and the new vicar had asked his

71

parishioners to contribute items that might be useful to those who had so little. Consequently, the following morning found Claire, Liam, Simon and Elise climbing into the O'Rourke's hot stuffy attic to look for donations.

Elise exclaimed with delight when she saw all the furniture that was crammed into the low-ceilinged space. "This will be perfect," she announced. "According to the vicar, some people are living with boxes instead of furniture."

Simon and Liam looked at each other. The furniture was massive. Liam said, "This stuff is heavy, Elise. And huge. It will never fit into a poor workman's cottage."

"The vicar will apportion it out. No one family will get it all," she said reasonably, as she studied a large tallboy and shook her head. "How ugly it is." She turned to Simon. "This is the furniture that was in the cottage when we arrived. I replaced it over the years with furniture in the French style. So much more agreeable. I have never liked your massive English designs."

"It's not very attractive," Simon agreed, as he looked at the heavy chairs, sofas and tables that were crowded together.

Liam said, "When we replaced it, the delivery people moved these 'massive English' pieces to the attic. Not Simon and me."

Elise's lovely face clouded. "I am asking too much of you."

Simon said gamely, "I'm sure we can move it, Mrs. O'Rourke."

Daniel sighed. If his wife wanted him to move it, move it he would.

By the time Liam and Simon had finished wrestling the heavy furniture down the steep, narrow attic stairs, out through the house and onto the drive, they were filthy and sweaty. Nancy was waiting with cool lemonade, and the two of them drank the entire pitcher while standing in the kitchen.

"At least someone is picking the stuff up," Simon said, as he and Claire went out to the driveway to see if the church wagon had come while they were inside. He pushed his hair back off his forehead and looked at the results of his labor, all spread out on the gravel drive.

They had brought out: a large, heavy table with six chairs; two old carved bedsteads; two sofas, a buffet; four end tables (all of them different); a huge stuffed chair; two wing chairs; an enormously tall oak chest, which had taken them forever to maneuver into position so it would go down the stairs; and a wardrobe. Elise had added to the furniture a collection of pots and pans; some place settings of china; old wool blankets; sheets, and two mattresses.

Claire was asking Simon about his trip into Cambridge when a farm cart came down the road and stopped in front of the drive. Simon recognized Jack Stepney, the driver of the cart, as one of Welbourne's tenants. Jack didn't recognize Simon at first, and when he offered to help Jack load the cart, he accepted. "This stuff is heavy," he said, as he and Simon lifted the sofa into the back of the cart. "Did a slim lad like you get it all out here by yourself?"

Simon laughed, his teeth white in his dirty face. "Mr. O'Rourke and I did the job. It was much harder getting it out of the attic than onto this cart, believe me."

It was the cut-glass aristocratic accent that gave him away. Jack peered at the face beneath the dirt and the tangled hair. It was not a face you could mistake. "God Almighty," he said. "You're Lord Woodbridge!"

Claire, who had been standing by quietly, spoke up. "He is indeed, Mr. Stepney. And a strong lad he is too. Let me carry the pots and blankets while you two toss in the heavy stuff."

"Aye, Miss O'Rourke," the farmer said. Then, to Simon, "If you'll take one end of the table, Lord Woodbridge, I'll take the other."

"Right," Simon said.

The cart was loaded and Jack drove off, treasuring the tale he would have to tell at the local pub come Saturday night.

\*

Claire and Simon repaired to the wide swing in the garden that Liam had put up years ago for his wife and daughter. When they were sitting side by side under the shade of the spreading elm, Claire said, "Tell me—what did you learn in Cambridge?"

"I found out I was right. We don't need the permission of our parents to marry in Scotland. All that's needed for a legal marriage there is that we be at least sixteen, which we are, and that we state our intention to be husband and wife in front of two witnesses."

"That's all?" She stared at him in disbelief.

"That's all," he assured her. "I read the law very carefully."

She nodded slowly. "That means we have to get to Scotland. Have you figured out how to do that?"

"I bought us tickets on the London to Edinburgh Royal Mail. We get on the coach in Cambridge and off in Carlisle. In Carlisle we'll hire a carriage and drive across the border to Gretna Green. And—wait until you hear this, Claire—in Gretna Green they've made a business out of marrying young English couples that can't get their parents' permission! They have priests and witnesses and places for newly married people to spend the night. Once we get there we won't have to arrange a thing."

Her face lit with her beautiful smile. "You're so smart, Simon. You found all that out in just one visit to Cambridge?"

Simon allowed himself to bask for a moment in her approval. Then he delivered the bad news. "It's close to three hundred miles from Cambridge to Carlisle—about thirty-eight hours of straight driving. The mail coach makes some stops, but only to change horses and drivers. We're going to be stuck in the coach for pretty much the entire time."

"It sounds ghastly," Claire said cheerfully.

"It will be," he agreed.

"Something to tell our children."

They grinned at each other.

"When do we leave?" she asked.

"Day after tomorrow. The mail coach gets to the George at 8:30 in the morning. I can get away without any problem, but it won't be so easy for you. Can you think up an excuse for your parents?"

"I'll tell them I'm spending the night with Charlotte. I've done it before, so they won't be suspicious."

"Are you going to go to Charlotte's, or do you want to meet me and we can set off for Cambridge? That would be easier."

She frowned thoughtfully and shook her head. "My father always drives me right to Charlotte's front door. I'm going to have to spend the evening there and escape sometime during the night. Can you fetch me at the squire's?

"Yes. I'm going to hire a horse and carriage in Newmarket to take us to Cambridge. I can come by the squire's. We'll drive directly to the George. That way we'll be certain not to miss the coach."

He paused, then pushed the swing a little with his foot, saying, "Will you have to tell Charlotte what you're doing? Can you get away without her knowing?"

Claire tilted her head as she thought. "I don't see how I can do that." She bit her lip. "I'm going to have to get Charlotte to lie for me, Simon. There's no other way this will work."

Simon frowned. "Can you trust her to do that?"

"Charlotte is my friend. She'll help me."

"Are you sure? If she tells, they'll separate us for sure."

They were silent as they contemplated this horrible thought. Then Claire said, "Charlotte won't tell. She may refuse to help me—which I don't think she will—but she would never betray me. I'm sure of that."

He nodded, taking her word for it. He had no choice, really. No one cared what he did, but Claire's parents watched over her carefully.

Claire leaned back, hands on the swing's ropes, and contemplated the cloudless sky. "This is what I'll do. I'll pack a bag—I always pack a bag when I spend the night with Charlotte—and my da will drive me to Winsted. We'll have dinner with the family, and Charlotte and I will pretend to go to bed. When everyone is asleep in their rooms, I'll sneak out and meet you where the Winsted road meets the path that runs down to the orchard. How does that sound?"

He didn't like it. He didn't like the idea of her sneaking around by herself in the dark. Liam would murder him if he ever found out. For some reason, it never occurred to him that Liam would also murder him for eloping with Claire.

"I suppose it will be all right," he said reluctantly.

"Do you have a better idea?"

"No. I don't."

She nodded and looked toward the house. "I feel terrible doing this to my parents, Simon. They're going to be so worried when they learn I've disappeared."

"I know and this is what I thought I'd do. I'll write a letter to your father explaining what we've done. I'll even tell him we're on the mail coach so he'll know we'll be safe. Every mail coach carries an armed guard, and highwaymen keep far away from it. I'll give it to Jem, one of the footmen who is a friend of mine, and tell him to deliver it tomorrow afternoon. I'll also tell him that I've asked my Uncle Richard to come to Carlisle and bring us back to face my father."

"Will Mr. Jarvis do that? Will he stand by us?"

"I'm sure he will. He despises my father and he feels guilty for neglecting me. He'll help us."

Claire looked down at her hands, now clasped in her lap. "What about my father? Do you think he'll lose his job?"

"Claire, the Welbourne Stud is the apple of my father's eye, and your father is the heart and soul of the operation. He'll never let Liam go to another owner. I'm sure of it."

This sounded like the truth.

"All right," she said. "I'll talk to Charlotte and let you know what she says."

The happy trill of Elise's laughter floated out to the garden. Simon's mouth tightened. "I don't like going behind your parents' backs like this, you know. They have always been so good to me."

"They love you," Claire said. She smiled. "They'll get over it, Simon. I know they will."

# CHAPTER TWELVE

When Charlotte first heard Claire's plan, she was appalled. "You can't be serious about this, Claire. Please tell me you're making this up."

The girls were sitting on a bench in the pretty topiary garden behind the squire's manor house. When Claire first asked if she could stay overnight, Charlotte had been delighted. When she learned the real reason behind Claire's request, however, she changed her mind.

Claire said earnestly, "I'm not funning, Charlotte. Simon and I have loved each other for years. All we want in life is to be together. This trust fund is like a gift from God. It means we'll have enough money to live on. But if we don't elope, we'll have to wait until Simon is twenty-one! That's *years*, Charlotte!" Her voice cracked a little. "Simon will be at school in Oxford, and I'll still be living home with my parents. You must see we can't do that! We love each other too much. We want to be together the way married people are. Can you understand that, Charlotte?"

Charlotte wasn't sure how she felt about Claire's passionate plea. She had always been jealous of Claire's friendship with Simon, had always known Simon was more important to Claire than she was. But she had never imagined that they might be in love! It changed the way she saw them, and it was confusing. She said, "I never thought of you and Simon in a romantic way. I thought you were just friends—the way you and I are friends."

Claire took Charlotte's hand in hers. "We're not friends the way you and I are. We want to be married; we want to sleep in the same bed. Can't you understand how cruel it is to keep us apart?"

Charlotte felt herself turn red at the words "sleep in the same bed." She looked around to make certain they were alone. "Have you kissed?"

"Of course we have."

"Oh." Quite suddenly she could imagine Simon and Claire kissing and she turned red again. "My goodness."

Claire took Charlotte's other hand into hers and turned her so she was facing Claire. "Please, Charlotte, will you help us? All you need to say in the morning is that I was in the bed next to you when we went to sleep. You never heard me get up. You're shocked to your very soul that I disappeared. I never said a word to you about anything." She squeezed Charlotte's hands. "You're my *best* friend, Charlotte. When Simon and I are married you'll still be my best friend. And just think—one day he'll be an earl and I'll be a countess. You can spend all the time you want at the abbey. Think how much your mother will love that!"

Charlotte looked into Claire's imploring brown eyes. Claire had said she, Charlotte, was Claire's best friend. Simon might be her husband but Charlotte would always be her best friend. Those were the two words that decided Charlotte. "Of course I'll help you," she said. "You're my best friend, after all."

Claire reached out and drew Charlotte into a hug. "I knew I could count on you!"

Charlotte laughed, and when the girls separated, she asked simply, "What do you want me to do?"

*

Their plan went smoothly. As expected, Liam drove Claire and her small bag of clothes over to Winsted, where she had dinner with the family. Geoffrey had gone to visit a school friend for a few days, so he wasn't home. Mrs. Weston was full of information about the vicar's charity collection and how many people would be helped, and the squire complained as usual about poachers. Mrs. Weston speculated on whom the vicar, who was young and single, might marry.

"He's not rich, of course, but the living is decent, and he is a gentleman," Mrs. Weston commented. "Louisa Merton would suit him very well. She's a sweet girl and the vicar would be a good match for that family."

Unspoken was the understanding that the charitable young vicar would not be a suitable match for Charlotte, who could certainly look higher.

After dinner the squire went to his library and the women gathered in the drawing room. Charlotte played a new piece she had been practicing, and Mrs. Weston described in detail a visit she had made to a local woman whom the girls scarcely knew. Tea was brought in early and Claire and Charlotte went upstairs to bed.

Charlotte had a large four-poster in her room, and she and Claire shared it when she stayed over. "Better get in on your side and make it look as if you slept there," Charlotte said, her voice lowered as if she feared being overheard.

"Good idea." Claire took off her shoes, climbed in and pulled up the covers. She proceeded to roll from side to side, mussing the bedclothes.

"Stop!" Charlotte said, laughing. "We don't want it to look as if we were wrestling."

Claire slipped out of the bed. "How shall we do this, Charlotte? What is the best way for me to get out of the house?"

Charlotte said, "Luckily, I remembered this afternoon that John locks all the doors before he goes to bed. One must have a key to open them from the inside as well as the outside."

Claire stared at her in horror. "Are you saying I won't be able to get out?"

"No, silly. I'm saying it's a good thing I remembered. I got you a key that opens the door into the kitchen garden. It hangs on a hook in the butler's pantry and I stole it just before you came." She went to the small table that was set in front of the fireplace and picked up a single key attached to a cord. "Here it is. When everyone's in bed you can sneak downstairs, unlock the door and escape into the kitchen garden."

Claire thought for a moment. "Won't they suspect something, though, when John can't find the key?"

"John has his own set of keys. He won't know the key is missing from the butler's pantry. After you open the door, you must leave the key on the ground just outside the door. I'll sneak down later, collect it, lock the door and return the key to the pantry."

Claire regarded Charlotte with admiration. "How clever you are, Charlotte. You make a splendid conspirator."

Charlotte flushed with pleasure.

The two girls moved at the same time into a tight hug. Claire said, "You are the best friend anyone could ever have. I love you so much. Thank you, Charlotte. Thank you for helping us." Tears stung her eyes and she sniffed. She dropped her arms and stepped away, attempting a smile. "I'll name our first daughter Charlotte. I promise."

"Oh Claire!" Tears were running down Charlotte's cheeks.

"Are you certain you're doing the right thing? You and Simon are going to be in so much trouble."

"I'm certain." Claire's voice steadied. "As long as we're together we can face anything. Please don't worry about me. And, if I have to, I'll swear on a bible that you had nothing to do with my escape."

Charlotte found her handkerchief and began to wipe her tears away. "You'll always be my best friend, Claire. Always."

"And you mine. Thank you, Charlotte. Thank you so very, very much."

\*

Charlotte's plan, well thought out and simple, worked beautifully. Sometime after midnight Claire kissed Charlotte goodbye and, with her bundle of clothes in one hand and a candle in the other, she crept quietly down the manor's back staircase. She knew this house as well as her own, so she went directly to the kitchen garden door and inserted the key Charlotte had given her.

The door opened easily, and she bent to put the key directly in front of it so it would be easy to find. The kitchen garden was dark, but Claire waited until she was at the end of the center path before she lit her candle. With the candle's help she was able to find the path to the gate.

The summer air was warm and the sky was filled with stars. She inhaled deeply and looked up at the heavens. *Please bless us, dear Lord,* she said quietly, her words a breath on the soft breeze. *We mean harm to no one. We only want to be allowed to love each other. I promise we will do everything we can to be the sort of people you want us to be.*

At the end of the drive she turned right on the country road in front of the squire's manor. Somewhere an owl hooted, and a small animal scurried across the road in front of her. The woods on either side of the road were dark, mysterious, and filled with rustling life. Claire thought it was very beautiful to be out in the dark like this. Almost spiritual.

She reached her meeting place with Simon more quickly than she had imagined. When she first turned into the orchard road she saw nothing, but then, out of the darkness, came Simon's voice.

"Is that you, Claire?"

"Yes. Where are you?"

"Here." He had her in his arms and was kissing her desperately. "I've been so afraid something would go wrong. So afraid you might be accosted on the road. So afraid..."

She reached up and put a finger on his lips. "There's nothing to be afraid of, Simon. I'm here and I'm perfectly safe. Charlotte was magnificent. She even stole the key I needed to get out of the house."

He laughed. He was still holding her and now he bent his head to kiss the top of her bare head. "I hope you have a bonnet with you. It will look very odd if you don't have a hat."

"I have a bonnet tucked into my bag."

"Good."

"So what do we do now?"

"We drive to the George outside Cambridge and wait for the mail. They'll never give us a room this late, so we'll have to sit in the waiting room."

She picked up his hand and held it to her cheek. "And I was looking forward to sharing a room with you so much."

He caressed her cheek and turned her face up to his. His white teeth shone in the moonlight as he said with a grin, "We're going to do this, Claire. We're going to get married!"

"Yes," she said, answering with her own radiant smile. "We most certainly are."

# CHAPTER THIRTEEN

Simon and Claire reached the George several hours before the mail coach was due to arrive. Simon left his hired horse and gig at the inn, having previously made arrangements for the livery stable in Newmarket to retrieve their property.

Even at such an early hour, the George was busy. The two of them sat on a bench in the large waiting room, their bags at their feet. When the taproom opened at six, Simon went to purchase some food in case they didn't have a chance to eat before they reached Carlisle. He put their bags on either side of Claire to make sure no one would sit too close to her while he was gone.

The waiting room had begun to fill up, and Claire was the only female. A tall, broadly built man with a large mustache and small black eyes sat on her bench, with only Simon's bag between them, and tried to start a conversation. Claire, speaking politely, told him that his seat belonged to her escort. The man looked around ostentatiously and said, "I don't see nobody."

To her relief she saw Simon coming toward her. "Here he is now," she said. "I see an empty seat over there. Perhaps you ought to take it before someone else does."

The man swung around and saw Simon, who was carrying a paper sack in his left hand. Claire said, "This man was just leaving."

The man's quick glance took in Simon's youth and he made a disparaging sound. "These seats is open to everyone," he said.

Simon looked the intruder up and down with cold eyes. "This seat is taken," he said in the cut-glass accent of the true aristocracy. "I suggest you find another."

The man hesitated, then stood up, mumbled something to Claire about "begging her pardon for the intrusion," and effaced himself. Simon moved his bag to the now-empty seat and sat down beside her, the sack on his lap. "I bought some bread and two pasties. They'll have to do until we reach Carlisle."

Claire, who was far too excited to be hungry, just nodded and said, "Good idea."

They sat on the bench for two more hours before the blast of a horn announced the arrival of the mail coach. Simon picked up both cases, and they walked together toward the stable yard. The horses being taken out of harness were breathing hard, and grooms led them away toward the stable. The mail guard, whose job was to warn coaching inns of their approach by blowing the horn, stood watching as a team of fresh horses was hitched up. He was an impressively large man, splendidly dressed in a scarlet coat with blue lapels and gold trim. He was equipped with two pistols and a blunderbuss and would stay with the coach for the entire trip, riding on the back.

Once the new horses were in harness, the guard beckoned to the four waiting passengers. Accompanying Claire and Simon were two middle-aged men. They gallantly insisted that Claire must have the place facing forward, so she and Simon settled themselves on the thinly padded seat. Their bags had been stowed in the small luggage space next to where the mail was kept.

Claire had just made herself somewhat comfortable when the new coachman came running out of the inn and climbed up to the front seat. They heard him call to the horses and the coach started forward. Claire's heart pounded with excitement. They were on their way!

*

When the four passengers had been riding for a short time, the two men introduced themselves. One was a country solicitor and the other owned a profitable store near Sheffield. Once they had finished speaking they waited politely for Simon to reply.

Simon obligingly related the story he had created to explain their presence on the coach. He and Claire were brother and sister, he said, and they were returning home to Carlisle to attend a funeral. They were taking the mail because it was the fastest way to reach their destination.

The thin, gray-haired solicitor looked at Claire and said, "I am sorry to hear of your loss."

Simon answered, "Thank you."

The heavy-set man with shrewd hazel eyes said, "You don't look like brother and sister."

Simon tried to squash the conversation by looking taken aback by this rudely personal observation, but Claire replied inventively, "We have different mothers, you see. But we never think of that, do we, Simon?"

"No," he said crisply, every inch the offended noble. "We don't."

The trip to Carlisle was long and exceedingly uncomfortable. The coach made sixteen stops to change horses, to leave off the mail they were carrying, and to take on the outgoing mail. Passengers got off and other passengers took their place. There was no time to eat a meal at the coaching inns; they only had time to use the inn's necessary and return to their seats. When the coach passed through towns and villages that were not scheduled stops, the guard threw out the bags of incoming mail, then grabbed the bags of outgoing mail from the local Postmaster, who had been alerted to their nearness by the mail guard's horn.

None of the other passengers were females, and Simon didn't like the way some of the men looked at Claire. But Simon had been prefect in a public school, and he'd perfected a look that could stop a grown man dead in his tracks. The men who tried to make Claire the object of their gallantry took one look at the expression in Simon's eyes, and abruptly ceased their attentions.

Claire slept for part of the way, her head pillowed on Simon's shoulder, but he was very conscious of being Claire's protector and maintained his vigilance, even when all the other passengers were dozing.

Thirty-eight hours after they had boarded, the coach pulled into the Coffee House Inn, the coaching inn on the main road outside Carlisle that was their destination.

# CHAPTER FOURTEEN

It was after midnight when Simon and Claire climbed out of the mail coach and collected their bags from the guard. The two other passengers were going on to Edinburgh and, as Simon turned to help Claire down from the coach, one of the passengers winked at her and said, "Good luck. I hope they don't catch you before you make it to Gretna Green."

Simon frowned and Claire stared in surprise. The passenger grinned and, after a moment, she smiled back and said, "I hope so too."

Simon took her arm as they went into the inn, which looked like every other inn they had seen on their journey. There was a bar and kitchen to the right of the door, and a table where the landlord stood greeting the new customers as they entered. Simon stopped at the table and asked for a room for himself and his sister.

The landlord, a tall skinny man with a long hooked nose and scraggly hair, looked them over with a sapient eye. Ignoring Simon's comment about his "sister," he asked, "Headed for Gretna Green, are you?"

Simon's mouth set, then he sighed and gave up. "Yes, we wish to go to Gretna Green. But we've just spent forty hours on the mail coach and we need to rest first. Do you have a room available?"

"That we do," the landlord assured him. "How were you planning to get to Gretna tomorrow? It's a good sixteen miles from Carlisle."

"I'm planning to hire a horse and carriage," Simon replied.

The landlord said, "There are always drivers with gigs here at the inn on the lookout for young folk wanting to go to Gretna. I can have a driver here early tomorrow morning if you want."

Simon felt a wave of relief wash over him. One problem solved. "Thank you," he said.

The landlord said curiously, "So why're a pair of nobs like you running away from your families?"

Simon exchanged a quick look with Claire, then said easily, "Oh, we're just like all the other couples who come here. We wish to be married."

The landlord shook his head. "Happen I'll see at least one of your fathers by late tomorrow. Howling with rage he'll be, if what I've seen in the past is anything to go by."

Simon thought unhappily of Liam's anger and disappointment. Then Claire took his hand as she said defiantly, "'What God has joined together let no man put asunder.' That's what the bible says. And the law says it too. Our fathers can rage all they want, but they can't undo a legal marriage."

"Oh, the marriages Mr. Elliot performs at Gretna are legal enough." The landlord looked Claire up and down. "You'd best consummate the marriage quickly, though, otherwise it can be annulled."

Infuriated by that look, Simon said in a voice as cold as arctic ice, "About that room?"

The landlord took a step backwards and when he spoke again his voice was respectful, "If you will come with me, I'll get you the key. And I'll relieve you of some of your money as well."

By the time Simon opened the door to their room, the two of them were staggering with exhaustion. He dropped the cases and turned to Claire, who had started to undo her dress. "I am going to crawl into that bed and sleep," she announced.

He was so exhausted he scarcely noticed her dishabille. He glanced around the room and said, "I'll take the chair."

She flashed him a look. "Don't be an idiot. Sleep in the bed with me. We're neither of us in a condition to do anything else tonight."

Simon gave her a crooked smile and admitted, "I could sleep standing up like a horse, but that bed does look good."

Claire stepped out of her dress and draped it over the plain wood chair standing against the wall. Clad in just her petticoat, she climbed into bed and pulled up the blanket. "Good night," she said to Simon, and closed her eyes. She was asleep before he crawled in beside her.

*

Claire was the first to awaken. They had left the window open and the sun was beaming a ray of light directly onto Simon's sleeping face. She looked at him and felt her heart turn over. Pale silver stubble showed on his cheeks, and his hair was ruffled and hanging over his forehead. A dusting of silvery hair covered his bare chest. He was so tired that even the sun on his face hadn't awakened him.

Claire slid carefully out of bed and looked at the dress she had draped over the chair last night. She had worn that dress for almost two solid days, and it looked it. She took a fresh sprig muslin frock from her case and carelessly stuffed the old one in. By the time she turned around to face the bed, Simon was awake and blinking in the sunlight.

"What time is it?" He rubbed his head, further mussing his hair. Claire hoped that, if they had a daughter, she would have Simon's hair.

"I think about seven," she said.

He yawned hugely. "I'll dress and we can get some breakfast."

Poor Simon. Suddenly Claire felt very motherly. "Did you get any sleep at all on that trip?"

"A little," he said.

Claire didn't believe him.

His blue eyes gazed seriously into her brown ones. "Claire, I don't think I've ever been this hungry in my entire life."

She gave him a tender smile. "Get dressed, and we'll go downstairs for breakfast."

*

They were stuffing themselves with eggs and sausage when a sturdy-looking young man with sandy hair and freckles approached. "I be Joe Mason and I heard you're lookin' to get to Gretna Green."

Simon put down his fork. "That's right. Can you take us?"

"Yep. That's why I'm here. My uncle marries people in Gretna. Do you be wantin' his services?"

"Yes," Simon said. "We want to be married as quickly as possible."

"Well, my uncle can do the job for you."

Claire continued to eat while Simon and Joe discussed money. Joe left to get his chaise and horses, and Claire said to Simon, "Why did you ask him to wait and return us here? I thought there were rooms in Gretna Green."

He was a little embarrassed as he answered, "I've been thinking... I don't want to spend my wedding night with you in a bed where who knows how many other people have spent theirs. I'd rather stay here at the inn. It's more...respectable."

"Oh," she said, deeply touched by his sentiment.

He sighed. "Wouldn't it be perfect if we could take a wedding trip? We could drive all around Scotland, just the two of us."

"It would cost too much money," Claire said regretfully. "And my parents would be too worried."

"True." He gave her a rueful look and admitted, "I've already spent almost half the allowance money Uncle Richard gave me."

Claire reached her hand across the table and he took it into his and held it tightly. She said fiercely, "Let's concentrate on getting married. Once we do that, we'll be bound together by a tie no one can break. Ever."

He raised her hand to his lips, opened it, kissed her palm and folded her fingers over the kiss. He said very softly, "I love you with every part of my being."

Something deep inside her trembled at the kiss, at the tone of his voice. "And I love you the same way," she whispered.

As they looked at each other, the noise and bustle of the inn faded into silence. For a brief, out of time moment, there was only the two of them, holding hands, looking deeply into each other's eyes and seeing love.

"We've always belonged to each other," Claire said softly. "We're just making it legal."

He nodded, blinked, and said, "I had better reserve a room for us before we leave."

She took her hand back. "Yes." She smiled at him as the excitement bubbled up inside her. "I am so happy, Simon!"

He was looking serious. "I am too. And I will be even happier once we have that paper in our hands." He regarded her empty plate. "Have you had enough to eat?"

"Yes."

"Then we had better be going."

They stood and Simon took her arm as they went to reserve a room for the coming night.

# CHAPTER FIFTEEN

Joe Mason and his team of horses moved briskly along the main road. It was a fine, clear day, with only a few high white clouds interrupting the deep blue of the sky. Claire sat on the single seat between Joe and Simon, her chest so tight with a mixture of excitement and fear she thought she might explode. She had to struggle not to keep glancing behind them, terrified she'd see one of their fathers racing after them. If the earl had come after them he would have taken his coach, and he wouldn't have had to stop to deliver the mail. Or her Da may have hired a coach.

She didn't say anything to Simon about her fear. He seemed quite certain that they had enough of a head start, and she was confident he was right. But still...and she glanced over her shoulder one more time.

After they had been on the road for several hours, they crossed a wooden bridge spanning a small river. As the horses came off the bridge onto solid land, Joe turned to his passengers with a grin. "Now ye're in Scotland."

Claire let out a long breath. "How much longer to Gretna Green?"

"About three-quarter mile."

And indeed it wasn't long until the horses turned into a narrow road, which led them into a small village. At first sight Gretna Green was not very prepossessing. In fact, it looked positively poverty stricken. Claire stared at the scattering of small clay houses in surprise; she had expected a village similar to the one at home. Before she could speak, however, Joe pointed his finger at a tiny church ahead on their left. "That's the kirk," he said. "The house next to it belongs to Mr. Elliot. He's the one who'll marry you."

"Will we be married in the church?" Claire asked.

"Naw, Mr. Elliot does the marriages at the inn."

Joe proceeded to steer the horses to the front of a stalwart looking brick building a quarter of a mile past the kirk and said, "If you and the lady go on inside, sir, I'll fetch Mr. Elliot for ye."

Simon jumped down from the high seat, lifted his hands, put them around Claire's waist, and swung her to the ground. When her feet touched the hard dirt road, Claire looked up the road again. Her heart was racing and she slipped her hand into Simon's as they walked up the few steps that led into the inn. The warmth of his fingers closing around hers felt reassuringly familiar.

The room inside was decorated like a parlor, with pictures on the walls and four chairs grouped in front of the empty fireplace. There was a taproom, but it was tucked into a corner, away from the main room. Even so, Claire could see several men sitting at a table.

"Would you like to sit down while we wait?" Simon asked her.

Claire looked at the dark, uninviting chairs and said, "No."

Simon nodded and the two of them stood in front of the empty grate, holding tightly onto each other's hand. Claire's heart was beating so loudly she could actually hear it. She shut her eyes and prayed: *Please, God, please, don't let anything stop us. We've come so far. We love each other so much...please...*

The inn door opened and a man came in, followed by Joe. As they approached, Claire looked warily at the so-called priest who was to marry them. She hadn't known what to expect, and, to her relief, he appeared to be perfectly ordinary in his black frock coat and fawn colored trousers. When he came up to them she saw a pleasant-looking man with a round face and trimmed brown beard. He exuded a sense of agreeableness she found reassuring.

"Well, well," Mr. Elliot said, after they had introduced themselves. "I imagine you youngsters are in a hurry and there's no reason to keep you waiting. Joe, you can be one of the witnesses, and if you'll fetch George from the taproom, he can be the other one." As Joe moved off, Mr. Elliot turned to Simon.

"While Joe is fetching the second witness, young man, you and I can discuss my fee."

"Of course," Simon said, as naturally as if he did this sort of thing all the time. "If you'll just tell me what you charge?"

"It depends." The priest cast a calculating look over them both, and Claire realized he was estimating how much he might be able to get.

"We're not rich, Mr. Elliot," she said resolutely. "We spent half of our money getting here, and we have to keep enough to get home."

Mr. Elliot lifted an eyebrow. "Mmmm. May I ask by what means you traveled?"

"We were passengers on the Royal Mail," Simon answered. "It was the quickest transport I could find. We got on in Cambridge and off in Carlisle, so the tickets were expensive."

"I see. So you're throwing yourselves upon my mercy, eh?"

The good humor never faded from the priest's face, which gave Claire some hope he would be reasonable.

Simon sighed. "I suppose we are, sir. I think I can spare twenty pounds. Will that do?"

*Twenty pounds?* Claire gave Simon an alarmed look. If Richard Jarvis didn't come that wouldn't leave them enough money to buy tickets on the Mail home.

Elliot saw the look. "All right, lad, I'll take your twenty pounds. Now follow me and I'll show you the room we use for weddings."

The priest took them to a door at the far end of the room, opened it and gestured them in.

The "wedding room" was small and stark. The only furniture it contained was a single square wood table set in front of a narrow fireplace, and a long trestle table placed under a small window. The square table held a thick open book, which Claire assumed to be a bible. Half of the trestle table was covered with individual stacks of paper, while the other half was bare save for a pen and inkstand.

"We might as well get the first part of the marriage business done while we wait for the witnesses," Mr. Elliot said, leading them toward the trestle table. He plucked a form from one of the piles, appropriated the only chair for himself, and sat at the table while they stood beside him. He picked up the pen and held it poised over the paper in front of him.

"Legal name, please, and place of abode," he said.

"Simon Charles Matthew Joseph Radley," Simon said. "Welbourne Abbey, Suffolk, England."

The priest raised his eyebrows at the address, but said nothing, filling out a line on the form in front of him.

"Claire Marie O'Rourke," Claire said next, "Hillside Cottage, Welbourne, Suffolk, England."

Elliot entered this information. "Your ages, please?"

"Eighteen," Simon said in a composed voice.

"Seventeen," Claire said.

"And you are both single persons?"

"We are," they chorused.

The door opened and Joe came in, followed by the man from the taproom who was to act as the second witness.

Mr. Elliot finished filling out his form, then the whole party moved to the square table upon which the bible reposed. Mr. Elliot stood in front of it and Simon, Claire and the witnesses stood before him.

"Do you have a ring?" Mr. Elliot asked Simon.

Claire's heart sank. A ring! Neither of them had thought of a ring!

Simon put his hand into his breast pocket and took out something. "Here it is." He glanced at Claire. "My mother left her jewelry to me. It's one of her rings."

Claire let out a long breath of relief.

Mr. Elliott took the ring from Simon and gave it to Claire. "Hold this until we need it," he said.

She took the ring and slipped it into the sash of her dress.

Mr. Elliott cleared his throat. "We shall now begin the ceremony.

Claire stood as straight as she could and looked into Simon's eyes. He looked gravely back into hers.

Mr. Elliot intoned, "Claire Marie, have you come here of your own free will and accord?"

"Yes," Claire replied, as firmly as she could.

"Simon Charles Matthew Joseph, have you come here of your own free will and accord?"

"Yes," said Simon.

*This is it,* Claire thought, and her heart began to pound in her chest.

The priest turned toward Simon. "Simon, Charles, Matthew, Joseph, do you take this woman to be your lawful wedded wife, forsaking all others, and keep to her as long as you both shall live?"

"I will," Simon said clearly.

Claire felt tears gathering in her eyes.

"Claire Marie, do you take this man to be your lawful wedded husband, forsaking all others, and keep to him as long as you both shall live?"

"I will," said Claire, blinking hard.

"Give the ring to Simon."

Claire plucked the ring from her sash and gave it to her almost husband.

Mr. Elliot said, "Now Simon, hand the ring to me."

Simon gave it to the priest, who then handed it back to him and instructed, "Now you may put it on the fourth finger of Claire's left hand."

Claire extended her hand. Simon put the ring on her finger, repeating after the priest, "With this ring I thee wed, with my body I thee worship, with all my worldly goods I thee endow, in the name of the Father, Son and Holy Ghost, Amen."

"Join your right hands please."

They reached out to each other, and Claire saw that Simon's eyes were bright with unshed tears too. Her throat felt tight but she managed to repeat after the priest, "What God joins together let no man put asunder."

Mr. Elliot lifted his hands in blessing. "Forasmuch as this man and this woman have consented to go together by giving and receiving a ring, I, therefore, declare them to be man and wife before God and these witnesses in the name of the Father, Son and Holy Ghost, Amen."

Claire smiled in relief. They had done it! They were married!

Simon stepped close to her and, bending, kissed her mouth.

"This is the best day of my life," he said, his voice low and not quite steady.

"Mine too," she whispered back.

Mr. Elliot shook Simon's hand and patted Claire's shoulder. They had to wait while he filled out the marriage certificates, one for his records and one for them. Then Joe took them back to the inn.

# CHAPTER SIXTEEN

Simon and Claire went decorously up the inn stairway to their room, their certificate of marriage safely in Simon's hand. As soon as they stepped inside he went to the leather folder he had carried in his travel bag and put the certificate into it. "It will be nice and safe there," he said with satisfaction. Then he straightened and turned to Claire.

Her brown eyes were huge. "I can scarcely believe it," she whispered. "We're married."

He grinned, encircled her waist with his hands, lifted her, and began to spin her around in a circle, laughing exuberantly. She braced her hands on his shoulders and laughed back down at him.

When he returned her to her feet, she looked up at him with eyes full of curiosity. "How do we start?" she asked.

There had been women in the town near Simon's school who offered opportunities for upper-class students to shed their virginity, but he had never taken advantage of them. He wanted to come to Claire as pure as he knew she would come to him. He looked at her now and felt such enormous tenderness, such gratitude that she had trusted herself to him, that he almost stopped breathing. Then he held out his hands and said, "Come here and kiss me."

*

Claire went eagerly into his arms and kissed him with all the love that was in her. He kissed her back so fiercely he pressed her head all the way back against his shoulder. After a while his lips moved from her mouth to the arch of her neck, then slowly back again to her mouth. She shivered as an amazing sensation rippled through her, from her mouth, to her abdomen then all the way down into her loins. When finally he lifted his head, her heart was pounding and her knees felt so weak that they wobbled and she would have fallen if he hadn't been holding her.

He said in a strangely husky voice, "Would it be all right if I took off your gown?"

Utterly stunned by that kiss, she managed to stutter her agreement.

Her simple, sprig muslin frock came off easily, dropping to the floor and pooling around her ankles. He put his hands on her waist and lifted her out of it, then stepped back to look at her. She was wearing only her petticoat and a thin cotton chemise, and at the look on his face her heart began to race even faster. She wet her dry lips with her tongue and said, "Now you take off your shirt."

He pulled his white muslin shirt out of his breeches and then over his head. He tossed it on the floor, his eyes never leaving her. His hair fell across his forehead in a spangle of silver gilt and she stepped back into his arms, lifting her face. As they kissed once more, she ran her hands up and down his back, feeling the strong muscles under the smooth skin. Just touching him this way made her breathing come even faster.

He surprised her by scooping her up and depositing her on the bed. Then he stretched out beside her, kissing her again, her mouth, her neck, then pushing her chemise down so he could kiss her breasts.

"You're so beautiful, Claire," he muttered. "Your skin is like silk."

The touch of his tongue on her nipples was sending liquid sensation pouring throughout her body. Her breath caught audibly and her fingers tightened on his back. He lifted his head to ask, "All right?"

"Yes!" she assured him huskily. "I like it."

"Oh God." His voice sounded like a groan. He inhaled deeply, sat up and ripped off his breeches. Then he was back, and she felt his hand on her drawers, pushing them down. She helped him get rid of them, and his fingers came up between her legs.

She stiffened at the touch. Claire had been brought up on a stud farm, and she knew what was going to happen next, but still the intimacy shocked her.

"Are you sure you're all right? Do you want me to stop?" Simon's voice was almost unrecognizable and she shook her head on the pillow. "No. No. I'm fine."

"Oh God. *Claire.*" He was panting. "I'll try to wait."

His fingers began to move again, and an amazing sensation began to emanate from his touch. Instinctively, she arched up against him, spreading her legs so he could go deeper.

"I can't wait any longer Claire," he said desperately.

"Go ahead," she said and opened her legs even wider so he could enter her. As he came in and began to move tentatively, a breathtaking tension started to build around him. She could feel liquid begin to flow where he was, making his passage easier. Her arms were around him and she followed his motion, totally concentrated on the feeling that was building inside her. Then he hit the barrier of her virginity.

"This might hurt," he said, his voice hoarse. Sweat was pouring off of him.

"That's all right, Simon." Her voice was almost as urgent as his. "I don't mind."

He groaned, reared back, and drove all the way in.

Claire's fingers dug into his shoulders. All of the wonderful tension was extinguished, replaced by a burning pain. She clenched her teeth so she wouldn't cry out. She felt him moving back and forth inside her, and dug her fingers tighter into his shoulders. At last he let out a sound she had never heard before, and collapsed on top of her. His heart was hammering so hard it made her breasts quiver. She held him close, burying her mouth in his hair, until his breathing and heartbeat finally began to slow.

*I gave him this,* she thought, feeling fiercely happy in spite of the pain.

Finally he lifted his head and looked at her, his eyes full of concern. "I hurt you. I'm sorry, Claire. Very sorry."

"It wasn't bad," she said, reaching up and smoothing her finger along his cheekbone. "We both know that a young mare's first time with the stallion is hard for her. It will get better. And I liked most of it very much."

His crystalline blue eyes smiled down at her. "I don't deserve you." He kissed her with great tenderness, and she guided his head to rest in the hollow between her neck and shoulder. They lay together like that for a long time, fulfilled and quiet and at peace.

# CHAPTER SEVENTEEN

Fortunately for Claire and Simon, Richard Jarvis was at his country home near Bedford when Simon's letter was delivered. Two hours later and he would have been on his way to London on business.

His butler brought Jarvis the letter while he was finishing up some accounts in his office. When he looked up and saw the butler in the doorway he said impatiently, "I thought I said I didn't what to be disturbed."

"I beg your pardon, Mr. Jarvis, but a groom has just arrived from Welbourne Abbey with a letter for you. It is from Lord Woodbridge and I thought you would like to see it before you left."

"A letter from my nephew?" Jarvis put down his pen. "You had better give it to me, Whiting."

The butler presented the silver salver upon which the letter reposed. Jarvis took it, saying, "Wait until I've read it, will you? There may be an answer."

"Certainly, Mr. Jarvis."

Jarvis unfolded the letter and read:

*Dear Uncle Richard,*

*By the time you receive this missive, Claire and I will have reached Gretna Green in Scotland where we plan to be married. I realize this will be a shock to you, but I love her more than anything in the world, and she loves me. My father would never agree to a marriage between us, so we have eloped.*

*I know we do not deserve your support, nevertheless, I am writing to beg you to help us. We are staying at the coaching inn in Carlisle, and I'm afraid I won't have enough money left from the 100 pounds you gave me to pay for the mail coach to take us home. Can you send me some more money? Or even a carriage? I do not want to subject Claire to the common stage, which is all I can afford at the moment.*

*We are both fully cognizant of how brazen such a request is, but I am hoping you will help us for the sake of my mother.*

*I have also sent a letter to Claire's parents so they won't worry, but I have yet to inform my father. Unfair as it may be, I am placing our future in your hands.*

*Your grateful nephew,*
*Simon*

Jarvis read the letter through twice. So that's what it was all about, he muttered to himself. I knew the two of them were up to something.

His eyes fell on the words, *for the sake of my mother,* and he shook his head. The young devil knew exactly how best to manipulate him.

He looked up and said to his butler, "Get me Hartly. Immediately."

"Yes, sir." The butler turned and left the room.

Hartly was Jarvis' coachman and Jarvis had made a quick decision to send him to Carlisle with Jarvis' carriage. He couldn't leave those idiot children stuck in an inn without money. For a few moments he contemplated the thought of going himself, but the thought of a long, fast drive over rough roads wasn't appealing. He would send Hartly to bring the children back here. Then he'd deal with them.

He read Simon's letter one more time and, reluctantly, he smiled. The young devil had pluck, he'd give him that. It would be interesting to hear what he had to say for himself when he arrived at Jarvis House.

*

Elise and Liam had been frantic with worry when the squire brought them the news of Claire's disappearance. They stood in their drawing room after the squire had left (with many protestations of apology and offers to help), and tried to decipher what could have happened.

"She had to have left of her own free will," Liam said. "If someone had come into the room to kidnap her, Charlotte would have heard something."

Elise's face was white with fear and shock. "Could she have gone downstairs for a book, or a drink, and encountered someone who shouldn't be in the house? A thief, perhaps."

Liam shook his head. "No thief would be idiot enough to try to rob the house of the local magistrate."

"Then Charlotte must know what Claire was up to," Elise said, her voice unusually stern.

"According to Weston she says she doesn't."

"She has to," Elise returned in the same uncompromising tone of voice. "Those two are as close as sisters. Charlotte would lie for Claire if Claire asked her to."

"She must be made to tell us, then," Liam said. "I'll go over to Winsted and get the truth out of her."

Elise put a restraining hand on his arm. "You can't just march in there and interrogate Charlotte, Liam."

His eyes were bright with anger. "Well, I am not going to just stay here waiting to hear that my daughter has been murdered. Or raped...." His voice broke and he pinched his lips together trying to compose himself.

Elise sat on the sofa, as if her knees had suddenly given out. She looked up at her husband, her hazel eyes wide. "I just had a thought... Liam, I wonder if Simon is gone too."

"Simon?"

"If something happened, and he needed help.... Claire would do anything for Simon. You know that."

"I'll ride to the abbey right now and find out."

Elise accompanied her husband to the door just in time to see one of the grooms from the earl's stable come riding up their lane. Elise grabbed Liam's arm and held it tightly as the groom dismounted and came to meet them.

"I have a letter for you, Mr. O'Rourke," he said. "Lord Woodbridge asked me to deliver it this morning."

Liam plucked the folded paper from the groom's hand, mumbled, "Thank you, Jeremy," and turned back into the house with Elise beside him. They stopped in the front hall and Liam unfolded the letter and read out loud:

*Dear Mr. O'Rourke,*

*By the time you receive this letter Claire and I will be on our way to Gretna Green to be married. We profoundly regret deceiving you and Mrs. O'Rourke, but we love each other deeply and there seemed no other way we could become husband and wife. My father would certainly forbid it, and I would be packed off to Oxford until I turned 21. We could not face that kind of separation again.*

*You and Mrs. O'Rourke have always been my true family and it grieves me to have deceived you. But Claire is my life, my other self, and she feels the same way about me. We could not bear three more years of separation. I hope and pray you will find it in your hearts to forgive me.*

*I have not written to my father. I doubt he even notices I'm gone. We hope to be home within the week; I'm sure my uncle will help us. Claire is very sorry for whatever anxiety her disappearance may have caused you, and hopes you will forgive her.*

*Respectfully,*
*Simon*

*P.S. I have the money from my mother's family to live on, so we do not expect you to support us.*

Liam looked at his wife, his eyes glittering with a mixture of astonishment and fury. "They're married! They eloped to Gretna Green! I can't believe it!"

Elise was equally astonished. "Married? Claire and Simon? I never thought..."

"I can't believe Claire would do this to us." Liam was staring at the letter as if it was poisoned.

Elise stretched out her hand for the infamous missive. "Let me see."

Liam gave her the letter and watched her face as she read. When she slowly folded it and gave it back to him he demanded, "Did you ever suspect this...this love affair?"

"*Non*. Never." She closed her eyes for a long moment, obviously thinking. When she opened them again she said, "And now I realize how stupid I have been. It was right there before me, but I never saw it. I thought of Simon as our son, and so I assumed that Claire thought of him as her brother." She shook her head slowly in disbelief. "The both of us were blind to what was between them, Liam. We saw what we expected to see, not what was there."

"That's because they wanted us to be blind." Liam was furious. "They deliberately deceived us. I blame Claire, but I blame Simon more. He didn't even have the decency to speak to me. Instead he talked my innocent daughter into an elopement. Gretna Green! Good God, Elise, it will be a huge scandal."

"Yes," Elise said quietly. "I fear it will be."

Suddenly Liam gasped and all the color drained from his face. "Elise! Do you think he has got her with child? Is that why they had to elope?"

"No." Elise's voice was deliberate and calm. "I do not think Simon would take advantage of Claire. He has far too much love and respect for you to do such a thing."

"He can't love and respect me that much if he's eloped with my daughter!"

"Come into the drawing room and sit down. We have to think about this. We have to decide what we should do."

When they were both sitting on the sofa, Nancy, who had kept to the kitchen ever since the squire's departure, came to the door and inquired, "Would you like some tea, Mrs. O'Rourke?"

"No, thank you Nancy. Not just now." Elise managed a strained smile. "Why don't you start tidying the upstairs?"

"Yes, ma'am."

"And close the door behind you," Liam barked.

The drawing room door closed soundlessly and Elise once more appropriated the letter, unfolded it and read these words aloud: *Claire is my life, my other self. And she feels the same way about me.*" She looked up at Liam. "They love each other. They love each other and they want to be together. Is that so bad?"

"Don't get too sentimental about this, Elise! They're seventeen and eighteen years old. They've never had a chance to meet other people. What do they know about love?"

Elise's hazel eyes were grave as she regarded her husband. "I was seventeen when I married you, mon amour. I knew what love was then, and in all these years my heart has never changed."

Liam was silent and, when he finally spoke, his voice was quieter. "We didn't elope. We were married with the permission of your parents."

"My parents wanted me to marry that dreadful old lord with no chin. They only agreed to allow me to marry you because I told them I would go and live with you without marriage if they didn't consent."

Liam's mouth dropped open as he stared into his wife's face. "You never told me that!"

She gave a very Gallic shrug. "I didn't want you to think ill of my parents."

He took her hands into his and looked deeply into her hazel eyes, now turned almost golden with emotion. "Would you have done it?" he asked huskily. "Lived with me without benefit of marriage?"

"Yes, I would have."

He drew her into his arms. "I love you so much," he said, his mouth buried in her hair. "So very much."

She pressed her cheek against his chest. "Don't you think that *our* daughter would know what it means to love a man?"

He sighed.

She said, "Do you think Richard Jarvis knew about this?"

"I doubt it." His voice was muffled by her hair. "Jarvis would never have gone along with a plan to allow his nephew to elope."

"Liam..." Her voice was tentative, "do you think the earl will dismiss you?"

He sat up, back to facing their immediate problem. "He would be perfectly within his rights to do so. But we have plenty of money saved and I can easily get another place if it becomes necessary. That's not what's worrying me right now." His face was grim. "Simon seems to think the earl will let him play love in a cottage with Claire. That's not going to happen. This is a very unequal marriage for Simon, and his father will do all he can to get it annulled.

"Can he get it annulled?"

"I doubt it." He gave her a sardonic look. "I'm quite certain the marriage has been duly consummated."

Elise wrung her hands. "There must be something we can do!"

"Not much, I'm afraid. My hope lies with Richard Jarvis. He's a powerful man and Simon seems to think he'll support the marriage."

Elise said, "Simon is like a son to us and Claire is our daughter. No matter what happens, they must always know that we will stand behind them. That is one thing we can do for them."

Liam sighed. "As usual, *mo ghra,* you are right. I just wish Simon had spoken to me. This was not the way to handle matters."

"Perhaps it wasn't, but they are young, Liam. Young people in love are not always wise."

"True." He gave her a somber look. "I'm going to have to tell the earl. Simon has not written to him and, while he might not love his son, he is certain to be distressed by his disappearance."

Elise sighed. "You're right."

"He might dismiss me on the spot when he hears about Claire."

"If we have to, we can always stay with the Westons until you find another job. But I agree the earl must be told. Simon was wrong not to write to him."

Liam got to his feet. "I'd better do it now, before I lose my courage."

She reached up a hand and he took it to pull her up to stand beside him. "You have the courage of a lion, *mon amour*. It's not you I worry about; it's those foolish children."

"I know. *Gretna Green!* There was no need to be so rash. Every newspaper in England will gobble up this scandal, and Claire will get the blame, not Simon. They'll say she seduced him."

"None of our friends will think that and those are the opinions that matter to me. To *us*, Liam."

For the first time since the letter had been delivered, he smiled. "As usual, you're right. I don't care what the damn English might think. The children are alive, they're healthy and that's what matters most."

"Amen," Elise said. "Now, go and get this duty over with."

He nodded, turned and left the room. A few seconds later she heard the front door open and shut.

*I hope the earl doesn't dismiss him,* Elise thought. *We're so happy here...we have so many friends...* She drew a deep breath and went into the kitchen to plan the menu for dinner.

# CHAPTER EIGHTEEN

When a grim Liam arrived at the abbey to inform Simon's father of their children's elopement, he was told the earl was away from home. Liam next asked to speak to Carstairs, the butler.

"I believe Mr. Carstairs is in consultation with Mrs. Willis, Mr. O'Rourke. If you will wait a moment, I'll see if he is available," John, the footman, told him.

It didn't take John long to return with an invitation to the housekeeper's room. Liam, who knew Mrs. Willis was exceedingly fond of Simon, felt comfortable speaking to her as well as to Carstairs, and followed John down the hallway.

The housekeeper's sitting room was quite comfortable, with a rocking chair in front of the fire and an upholstered sofa along one wall. Carstairs and Mrs. Willis had been in service at Welbourne since before Simon was born, and they knew each other very well.

As Liam entered the room, Mrs. Willis gave him a look of great anxiety. She was a woman in her sixties, with a large, determined nose, a narrow chin, and kind brown eyes. She asked immediately, "Please, Mr. O'Rourke, have you come to tell us something about Lord Woodbridge? We've just discovered he did not come home last night. That's not like him!"

"Yes, it's about Lord Woodbridge. I need to communicate with his lordship. Do you have his direction?"

"Yes, of course. He and Lady Welbourne left two days ago to pay a visit to Lord Aston in Wiltshire."

"Wiltshire," Liam repeated, calculating in his head how long it would take for a messenger to ride to Wiltshire.

Carstairs said hesitantly, "May I ask—is Lord Woodbridge at your house, Mr. O'Rourke? I must confess Mrs. Willis and I are quite worried about him."

"No, I am sorry to say that he is not at my house," Liam said. Then, hastily, as both servants looked alarmed, "But I can assure you he is safe."

"Thank God," Mrs. Willis breathed. She sat down in her rocking chair and gestured for the men to take the sofa.

Liam had not planned to tell anyone about the elopement except the earl, but, confronted by those two worried faces, he changed his mind "What I am about to say must be kept in this room."

Carstairs elevated his impressive hooked nose. "We do not tell tales, Mr. O'Rourke."

"I know you don't, and I know you are fond of Lord Woodbridge, so I will tell you the truth. He has eloped to Gretna Green with my daughter."

Stunned silence greeted this announcement.

Finally Mrs. Willis collected herself enough to ask, "Did they make it to Scotland? Are they married?"

"They may not be married yet, but, as there is no one on the scene to stop them, they will be shortly. And I have the fortunate task of telling his lordship what his heir has done with my daughter."

"Well." Some color returned to Mrs. Willis's cheeks. "I am glad of it," she said defiantly. "Lord Woodbridge loves that little lass and she loves him. She's good for him. I'm glad."

"It's all very well for you to think that way, Mrs. Willis," Carstairs rumbled in his deep, carefully enunciated voice, "but you can be sure his lordship won't. He will be livid."

"Yes, he will be," Liam said resignedly. "But he must be told. If I write a letter, will you see that it is delivered to Lord Welbourne in Wiltshire?"

"Of course, Mr. O'Rourke, of course."

Liam sat down at the small mahogany secretary in the corner of the room and accepted the paper and pen Mrs. Willis handed him. He wrote quickly, stating only the bare facts of the successful elopement and the imminent return of his son with his bride.

"See that it goes at once," he said.

"That I will," Carstairs replied, taking the folded paper from his hand.

Liam left the abbey through a back door, and rode slowly back to the cottage, his mind fixed on what the earl might do when he heard the news. He didn't doubt that Simon would stand up to his father and fight for Claire. The boy detested his father, but he didn't fear him. The problem was that Simon was still only eighteen years old, three years away from attaining legal status as an adult. Until then he was in his father's power.

One thing the earl would not be able to change was the validity of the marriage. It had been legally transacted in Scotland, and Scottish law was honored in England. The question was: would it be possible for Welbourne to separate husband and wife for three years? Liam had an unpleasant feeling they were all about to find out.

*

Five days after Simon and Claire had eloped, the Earl of Welbourne returned to his home. His fury was felt by everyone in the house, and by many others who worked on the estate. He raged at Liam for a full forty minutes before telling him to "*Get out of my sight before I do something I will regret!*"

"Well, he didn't dismiss me, *mo ghra*," Liam said to Elise when he returned to their cottage. "He was damned offensive, but it could have been worse."

Privately, Liam had decided that if the earl behaved as Liam was afraid he would, Liam would take Elise and Claire—and Simon, if he could—and find a position somewhere else. The man was poisonous. Liam felt infected just being around him. If Simon and Claire had to wait three years before they could be together, then they would have to wait. After some of the disgusting things Liam had heard pouring from the earl's mouth, he quite frankly never wanted to speak to the man again.

And so things stood at Welbourne as they waited for the return of the newlyweds, Simon and Claire.

# CHAPTER NINETEEN

It was a warm summer afternoon when the carriage carrying Simon and Claire turned into the drive of Richard Jarvis' country estate. The house was hidden from the road by a bank of old trees, but when it came into view a lovely old manor house built of mellowed brick was revealed. It reminded Claire of the squire's home of Winsted, which she had always loved. The surrounding lawn was perfectly cut, and a profusion of flowerbeds added brilliant color to an already attractive picture.

As soon as the carriage stopped, the front door of the house opened and a footman appeared. Claire instinctively exchanged looks with Simon as they watched him walk in a stately manner down the path to the carriage door. "Say a prayer," Simon muttered as he opened the door and jumped down.

"Good afternoon, Lord Woodbridge," the footman said with a little bow. "The steps will be here in a moment for Lady Woodbridge to descend."

*Lady Woodbridge!* Claire looked down at her rumpled dress and put a hand up to her long, tied back hair. She looked like a farmer's wife. What could she possibly find to say that would convince Simon's uncle that she was an appropriate bride for a future earl!

"We don't need the steps," Simon said, and took her hand as she jumped lightly to the ground.

"Mr. Jarvis will see you in the small salon," the footman announced and began to lead the way up the stone walkway to the house.

Claire glanced again at Simon as they walked together toward this vital meeting with his uncle. His expression was calm and confident, but a muscle twitched in his jaw and she knew he was as uncertain as she about what their reception might be.

The room they were shown into was bright, with sunlight streaming in through two tall windows. An ivory brocade sofa stood in front of the fireplace with two upholstered chairs on either side of it.

"Mr. Jarvis will be with you shortly," the footman said, and left without offering them any refreshment.

They sat on the sofa, very close to each other.

"I feel like a prisoner about to face the judge," Claire whispered.

Simon grinned, and just looking at that familiar smile made her feel better.

The door opened and Richard Jarvis came into the room. Simon and Claire stood up in unison and faced him.

"Welcome to my home," Jarvis said gravely.

"Thank you, sir," Simon returned. "And thank you for sending your coach for us. The journey to Scotland cost more than I thought it would."

Jarvis came to shake Simon's hand. Then, after a moment's hesitation, he bent to kiss Claire's cheek. The touch of his dry lips on her skin made Claire suddenly feel certain that he would help them, and she gave him her wonderful smile.

"It was far more comfortable than the mail coach," she said confidingly.

It was impossible not to respond to that smile and he smiled back.

"Sit down, sit down." He gestured to the sofa and, once they were seated, he took one of the chairs.

"So—you are married then?" Jarvis asked Simon.

"Yes, sir, we are. I have the certificate in my case."

"It was done in Gretna Green?"

"Yes."

Jarvis raised a sardonic eyebrow. "I imagine that must have been an interesting experience."

"It got the job done," Simon replied soberly.

"Yes, it did." Jarvis looked from Simon to Claire then back again to Simon. His voice was pleasant as he asked, "Well, now that you have accomplished your marriage, have you made any plans for your future?"

Of course they had talked about their future! Claire thought. But so much depended upon this man agreeing to help them. She had to restrain herself from putting a hand on Simon's leg to encourage him.

Simon said easily, as if it were a matter of minor concern, "I was rather hoping my father would allow us to live on his estate in Ireland. If you would agree to give me my allowance, I'm sure we will manage quite well."

Claire's eyes were glued to Jarvis' face. From his expression it was clear that Simon had surprised him. "My understanding is the estate in Ireland is a castle," he said slowly. "You would need a considerably higher sum to live in it than a hundred pounds a quarter."

They had discussed this, and Claire listened anxiously as Simon explained, "We don't plan to live in the castle, sir. We'll live in one of the attending cottages."

Jarvis' eyebrows rose. "I see." His voice was perfectly courteous as he continued his interrogation, "And what do you plan to do while you are living in this cottage? Grow potatoes?"

At this comment, Claire had to pinch her lips together to keep from replying. Simon, who was still managing to look cool and confident, said, "We can most certainly plant a vegetable garden."

He didn't seem at all intimidated by his powerful uncle, and Claire shot him an admiring look.

Jarvis leaned back in his chair and steepled his fingers in front of his mouth, looking at Simon over them. There was a long silence, and Claire had to fight hard not to show the anxiety that was gripping her.

At last Jarvis said, his voice more realistic than the uncomfortably pleasant tone he had hitherto employed, "Your father will never allow you to go to Ireland, Simon."

Simon disagreed. "I think he will, sir. I think he will be delighted to be rid of me. And his wife will encourage him to let us go. If I am tucked away safely in Ireland, they can pretend I don't exist and bring Charlie up as if he will be the heir." A note of passion entered his careful voice. "I wish he was the heir. I wish to God I could be just Simon Radley, with no title hanging over my head. If I was just an ordinary person I could get a job working in your bank, and Claire and I could marry and have a normal life like other ordinary people."

It was crystal clear that Simon meant every word he had spoken.

His uncle sighed. "You are not an 'ordinary person,' however. Like it or not, one day you will be the Earl of Welbourne, with all the power and responsibility that comes with such a title. Now, you wrote to tell me about the elopement, and you wrote to O'Rourke. Have you written to your father?"

"No, sir, I have not."

"You should have." Jarvis was very serious.

"I doubt he's even noticed I'm gone." Simon's voice was deeply bitter.

For the first time a flicker of emotion crossed Jarvis' face. "He may not love you, but you are still his heir. He won't like this unequal marriage, Simon. He may even try to get it annulled. You must prepare yourself for that."

Simon picked up Claire's hand and held it in such a strong grip it hurt. "I don't care what he likes or doesn't like. We're married and there are no grounds for an annulment."

Claire, taking courage from that hand crushing hers, spoke for the first time. "The earl has treated Simon abominably. The best thing that could happen to both of us would be to never have anything to do with him again!" Her temper flared every time she thought of Simon's horrid father and she added passionately, "He's an evil man. Mr. Jarvis. We know he'll want to separate us, but we won't let him!"

Simon shot her a quick smile, and turned back to his uncle. "I have some information about my father that I think you might find of interest, Uncle Richard."

"Oh? And what is that?"

"It appears that my father is rather deeply in debt."

Claire, who knew what Simon was going to say, sat perfectly still, her eyes fixed on Jarvis.

Jarvis said sharply, "How did you find this out?"

Simon flushed as he went on. "Just before we eloped I overheard a conversation between my father and our estate agent. They were in the library, and I had come to look for a book. I hesitated when I heard them talking, and I was about to go away when I realized what the conversation was about. So," he raised his chin and the color deepened in his cheeks, "I stayed where I was and listened. Mr. Halleck was talking about all the repairs that need to be done on the estate, and asking my father to authorize money to replace some roofs. And my father said...well, he told Halleck there was no available money for the estate, that he had debts that had to be paid first, and he didn't want Halleck bothering him again about the damn roofs or anything else to do with the tenants."

A fraught silence greeted the end of Simon's speech. Claire glanced at his face, then looked again to Jarvis, who still hadn't said anything.

"I'd heard something else earlier," Simon added. "I heard my stepmother accusing my father of running through both my mother's money and her own marriage settlement." He flushed as he realized how he must sound. "I can assure you, sir, I don't usually go around listening at doors."

"You have every right to know what your father is doing with your inheritance," his uncle said emphatically. "Tell me this, is Welbourne gambling?"

"I know he wagers a lot on horses. He does all right when he wagers on our horses, but he goes to all the race meetings, even when we don't have a horse running, and I think he bets heavily. Apparently he doesn't do so well on those bets." Simon leaned a little forward. "I've been thinking about this, Uncle Richard. That's the reason he's so furious the trust fund is coming to me and not to him. He needs the money to pay his gambling debts."

By now Richard Jarvis was incensed. Claire sighed with relief as she looked at his face. He would handle the earl for them.

Jarvis said grimly, "I will take care of this situation, Simon — and without touching your trust fund! James Radley will not get a farthing more of Jarvis money. Not One Farthing." He got to his feet and jerked the bell pull for a servant. "I'll have my housekeeper show you and Claire to your room. You'll stay here overnight and tomorrow the three of us will go to Welbourne. The earl has a lot to answer for, and he'll answer for it to me."

Simon glanced at her and she stood up with him. "Thank you, Uncle," Simon said.

A footman appeared at the doorway and Jarvis said, "Have Mrs. Emory show Lord and Lady Woodbridge to the green room." He turned to Simon. "Dinner will be at six thirty in the dining room. I will see you there."

"Thank you, Uncle," Simon said again, and Claire echoed his words.

The housekeeper took them up the stairs to a very pretty room that overlooked a rose garden. Their paltry luggage had already been placed inside. As soon as the door closed after the housekeeper, Claire flung her arms around Simon.

"It will be all right! Your uncle is going to help us! Isn't it a good thing that your father gambled away all that money?"

Simon's arms closed around her and she felt his lips on the top of her head. "And isn't it a good thing I eavesdropped on those conversations?" He sounded amused.

She snuggled her face into his shoulder. "God put you there. I really do believe that."

She felt him pulling the ribbon out of her hair. Free of its confinement, it spilled down her back, almost to her waist. He spoke softly into her ear, "Doesn't that bed look comfortable?"

She took her head out of his shoulder and looked up into his face. His eyes were narrowed and held a look she had come to know well in just a few days. She smiled. "It does indeed, my husband. Shall we try it out?"

"Oh definitely." And he picked her up and carried her over to the high, pillow-decked bed.

# CHAPTER TWENTY

After breakfast the following morning Claire and Simon ascended once again into Richard Jarvis' coach, this time with Jarvis himself accompanying them. The three passengers were silent during the drive, with Simon striving valiantly to hide from Claire how worried he was about meeting her father. Now that Simon had known the bliss of being with her, of waking in the morning to see her beautiful face on the pillow next to his, he could not, would not, be parted from her again. He hoped with all his heart that Liam would understand.

Unfortunately, it was his father, not Liam, who had the power. For the thousandth time Simon thought, *If only I wasn't so young!* He looked at his uncle sitting across from him in the carriage. Jarvis' eyes were closed and he looked as if he was dozing. Uncle *Richard may be a powerful man in the city of London,* Simon thought, *but he has no power over my father.* The only person who had power over the Earl of Welbourne was the king, and Simon hardly thought the king would be interested in his personal problems.

Simon closed his eyes and prayed with all his heart: *Please, God, let my father allow us to go to Ireland.* When he opened his eyes again, Claire was looking at him anxiously. He smiled at her and took her small, elegant hand into his.

"Don't worry, Simon," she said. "It will be all right. I get these feelings once in a while—Da says it's the Irish in me—but they always come true. We'll be all right, Simon. I just know it."

"I'm glad to hear that," Simon said, and tried to wipe the nervous look from his face.

\*

They stopped once for something to eat and were in Newmarket by early afternoon. By the time the carriage was rolling down the lane that led to the O'Rourke's cottage, Simon could no longer hide his anxiety about meeting Claire's father.

What would Liam say? Simon knew Claire's family had never suspected the true relationship between their daughter and the boy they had treated like a son. They had believed the two regarded each other as siblings, and Simon had to admit that he and Claire had done everything possible to foster that misunderstanding.

He had deceived the one man in the world he loved and admired. The man who had always stood by him, who had been the only father he had ever known. Liam would think Simon had betrayed him, and Simon wouldn't blame him if he did.

It would hurt Simon to his very soul if Liam turned on him. But even should that happen, Simon wasn't sorry for what they had done. Claire and he belonged together, and nothing could ever change that. Even if Liam hated him, he would not have done things differently.

Next to him Claire slid to the front of her seat and said happily, "We're here!"

Simon looked at her glowing face. She at least had no doubts about her reception. The blame for what they had done wouldn't fall on her. Nor should it. Simon knew he was the responsible party, and so would the O'Rourkes.

"Look, Simon," Claire said. "There's Mama!"

Simon glanced out the window and saw Elise, scissors in hand, standing next to the neat row of irises that marched across the front of the cottage.

"Wait until the horses stop and Jeffries can open the door for you," Jarvis said sharply, as Claire looked about to jump out of the carriage.

The horses stopped, Claire opened the door and jumped out. "Mama," she cried. "We're home!"

Elise dropped the scissors she had been holding and came running toward the coach. Claire ran toward her as well, and the two of them came together in a tight hug.

"Claire!" Elise kept saying. "It's you! It's really you!"

"It's so good to see you, Mama!" Claire pulled away so she could look into Elise's face. "I hope you weren't too worried. Simon did send you a letter. You got it, didn't you?"

"Yes, we got it, but of course we've been worried. Just imagining the two of you, all alone, heading for Scotland, was terrifying. On a public mail coach! I was petrified."

"Simon took good care of me, Mama," Claire assured her. She finally turned and saw Simon standing quietly ten feet away. "Simon, come and say hello to Mama," she said with a radiant smile.

Simon approached cautiously, prepared to be met with anger and reproach. Instead Elise opened her arms wide and said, "Simon! Thank God the both of you are safe." Relief flooded Simon's heart, his long legs covered the ground between them, then he was safe in Elise's arms.

"I'm sorry we frightened you," he said, his mouth next to her ear.

"And well you should be," she retorted. But her arms tightened, and he felt the knot that had been in his stomach ever since they left Jarvis House begin to loosen.

From behind him Richard Jarvis' deep, authoritative voice said, "I assume this lady is your mother, Claire?"

Simon stepped back and turned to his uncle. "I'm sorry, Uncle Richard. Mrs. O'Rourke, this is my uncle, Richard Jarvis. He was good enough to send his carriage to bring us back from Carlisle, and he has transported us here today as well."

Elise smoothed her somewhat disordered hair and smiled at the banker, holding out her hand. "Thank you for coming to the rescue of my children, Mr. Jarvis," she said.

"Let me assure you I did not assist in this elopement, Mrs. O'Rourke," Jarvis said. "My only involvement was to return them to you."

Elise took back her hand and collected herself. "My goodness, we can't keep standing here in the yard. Please, won't you come into the house, Mr. Jarvis. I'm certain you could use a cup of tea after so long a journey."

"Thank you, Mrs. O'Rourke, I could."

"Simon," Elise said. "Liam is at the farm. Could you find him and bring him home?"

When Elise spoke in the tone Simon and Claire had secretly designated as her *I am the daughter of the Comte de Sevigny* voice, you did not ask questions. "Of course," Simon said, hoping his dismay didn't show on his face. He would have much preferred to meet Liam while he was with Claire.

She gave him a sympathetic smile as she moved toward the house with her mother and Jarvis, but she didn't offer to accompany him. He was on his own, and he started off down the hill that would bring him to the stud farm with his chin up and his shoulders back, like a soldier going into battle.

# CHAPTER TWENTY-ONE

Simon found Liam in one of the barns watching the blacksmith put shoes on one of Fergus' most promising yearlings. Their old blacksmith had retired and left the business to his son, and Liam wanted to make certain the young man wasn't holding the horses' legs up for too long. He was so intent on watching he didn't notice Simon until Simon spoke his name.

Liam's head swung around and Simon looked back, trying not to look apprehensive.

"Simon!" Liam said. He looked over the boy's shoulder. "Where is Claire?"

"She's up at the cottage, sir. Mrs. O'Rourke sent me to fetch you."

Liam said to the blacksmith, "Carry on, Jem." Then, to the groom who was holding the colt's halter rope, "put him out in a paddock when he's done. Give him a chance to move around before you return him to his stall."

"Yes, sir," the groom replied.

Liam came over to Simon and put an arm around his shoulders. "Come along with me to the office, Simon. We have things to discuss."

Simon eyes closed in relief when he felt that strong arm encircle him. He said, "I know you must be angry we ran away, but it was my idea, sir. Claire's not to blame."

They stepped out of the stable and into the bright sunshine. Liam said, exasperation in his voice, "Whatever possessed you to elope? Why didn't you come to me first?"

The words poured out of Simon; it was so important to make Liam understand! "I didn't come to you because I knew there was nothing you could do to help us. My father would never allow us to marry, and, until I'm twenty-one, I'm under his power. Eloping was the only possible way to circumvent him." He glanced anxiously at Liam's profile. "He wanted to send me to Oxford, and

I couldn't bear being separated from Claire again. I was just so sick of school and boys and being away from home." Simon looked straight ahead, his mouth set hard, his voice a little unsteady. "And I'll admit it—I was afraid of him. If he ever discovered I loved Claire he would have done something terrible to separate us." His chin went up. "But we're legally married now, and there's nothing he can do about it."

They had reached the building that held Liam's office and Simon followed him inside. Once they were in the familiar room, Liam shut the door and took his usual chair behind the big, scarred old desk. Simon sat in his own usual seat and thought nostalgically of all the happy hours he had spent here with Liam talking about horses. He desperately wanted Liam to accept him and what he'd done.

Liam pushed a pile of papers away and regarded Simon, his expression very somber. "Something quite unexpected happened while you were gone, Simon, that is going to change your life. And Claire's life as well."

Simon had never seen Liam look quite like this. "What is it?" he asked in alarm.

"Your father is dead, dear boy."

Simon blinked. Had he heard correctly? "My father is dead?" he repeated in bewilderment.

"Yes. It happened two days ago."

Simon stared into Liam's eyes, the eyes that were so like Claire's. "How can that be? He wasn't that old. And he was perfectly healthy the last time I saw him."

Liam leaned down and took a bottle out of the bottom drawer of his desk. He poured a small amount into a glass, which had also come from his drawer, and handed it to Simon. "Take a dram, my boy. You'll need it."

Simon took the glass. It burned going down, and his eyes watered, but it did energize him. He blinked a few times and said, "That was pretty strong."

"Irish whiskey. The best." Liam poured a glass for himself.

Simon had never thought of his father as a mortal being. It had always seemed to him that the earl would be there forever, doing everything he could to thwart his son's happiness.

"I would be lying if I said I was sorry," he said now. He drank the last of the whiskey and stared into the empty glass. "But..." his voice trailed off.

"What is it boyo?" Liam asked gently.

Simon hesitated, then he almost whispered, "It's that now I'll never know why he hated me so much."

Liam reached out and put his hand on Simon's arm. "It wasn't your fault, Simon. It was some twisted thing in your father. There has never been anything wrong with you."

Simon managed a wobbly smile.

Liam leaned back in his chair and said, "He was shot to death, Simon. That's how he died."

Simon's eyes flew open wide. *"Shot? By who?"*

Liam finished his own dram of whiskey and said, "This is how it all happened. Once I knew you and Claire were safely out of reach, I sent a letter to the earl where he was staying in Wiltshire informing him of your elopement."

Simon held onto those words: *Once I knew you were safely out of reach.* Liam had wanted them to get to Scotland! He wasn't angry about the marriage. A tremendous feeling of relief swept over Simon. He heard Liam's voice going on and brought his attention back to his words.

"The earl came back to Welbourne in a roaring fury. I've never seen him so angry—not even when Elegant Lady got interfered with in the Oaks and didn't win."

As Simon knew, his father's anger at that particular moment in his life had been epic.

Liam continued, "According to the countess, they were having a late dinner when one of the footmen mentioned he had heard shots coming from the abbey woods. The earl said, 'Shots? Are those damn poachers daring to come into my own woods?'

"The countess said he was like a madman. He jumped to his feet and called for his gun."

Simon's face was stunned. "He called for his gun? My father went after the poachers himself? Why would he do such an idiotic thing?"

"I'm thinking he was in the mood to shoot someone, my boy, and he had been railing against those poachers for the entire summer. At any rate, his gun was brought and he strode out of the house, still in his dinner clothes, determined to aid in the capture. The countess tried to stop him, but he wouldn't listen."

Liam looked somber. "The poachers had guns of their own, of course, and in the exchange of fire, your father took a bullet in the chest. He lived only a few hours."

Simon sat in dazed silence, one thought going round and round in his head. My father is dead. My father is dead. He has no power over me anymore. He is dead and I am…

Simon's head lifted and he stared at Liam in horror. "But if my father is dead that must mean that I…that I…"

"You are the Earl of Welbourne, Simon. You have been for two days now."

It was all too much for Simon to take in at once. He looked up at Liam, who had always helped him, and said helplessly, "But I have no idea how to be an earl, Mr. O'Rourke. My father never shared anything with me."

"You're a smart lad, and you'll learn," Liam said. "Your father's solicitor and agent will help you. All of the servants at Welbourne will help you. Your uncle will help you, and so will Claire, Elise and I."

Simon felt his lips tremble and was horribly afraid he was going to cry. He fought a silent battle with himself, then managed to say with calm dignity, "Thank you, Mr. O'Rourke. Thank you for everything you have done for me over the years."

Liam grinned. "Since I'm now your father-in-law, do you think you could call me something more personal than Mr. O'Rourke."

"W-what do you suggest?" Simon wouldn't dare to come up with a suggestion of his own.

"Not 'Da,' that belongs to Claire. How about just plain 'Liam'?"

The incipient tears threated again and Simon clamped down hard. "I'd like that," his voice only a little emotional.

"I'd like that too." Liam sighed. "I hate to land you with this, Simon, but we're going to have to talk about your father's funeral. His body has been lying in the icehouse waiting for you to return home to make the decisions."

Simon was horrified. "I've never even been to a funeral. I have no idea what to do."

"According to Elise, who is the daughter of a Comte, it is going to have to be very elaborate with lots of mourning coaches in the cortege. She says the way he died is sure to cause speculation, as will your elopement and marriage. A properly solemn and respectful funeral will help to demonstrate your fitness to take over the duties of the Earl of Welbourne."

As Simon listened to what Liam was saying his chest tightened. How on earth was he to organize such a funeral? But a part of him also knew Liam was right, he was going to have to show the world that he and Claire were perfectly capable of assuming the duties required of the Earl and Countess of Welbourne.

"Has a death notice been sent to the papers?" he asked.

"Yes. The countess—er the dowager countess—sent a notice."

The two men looked at each other.

"Good God," said Simon in horror. "What am I going to do with my father's wife?"

"There is a will. You won't have to make any decisions until the will is read. That will take place after the funeral."

"And Charlie! What will happen to Charlie?"

"We'll know more after the will is read," Liam repeated.

He stood and pushed his chair back under the desk. "Come along, my boy, and we'll go back to the cottage to see how the women are doing with your uncle."

Simon followed his new father-in-law out of the stable, his head in a whirl. All he wanted to do right now was grab Claire's hand and hold it tight. It would be all right, he assured himself as he walked beside Liam up the path to the cottage. As long as he had Claire he could face anything. His teeth clenched; even his stepmother.

# CHAPTER TWENTY-TWO

The Earl of Welbourne's funeral was the largest event in the surrounding area since his marriage twenty years before. Over fifty coaches, all draped in black and carrying half the members of the Jockey Club, as well as noble friends of the earl from London, formed the funeral procession to the church. Simon sat in the first coach with Claire, Elise and Liam. Liam had wanted Elise to go without him. "You're the daughter of the Comte de Sevigny," he had said. "You're the one who gives status to Claire—not her horse trainer father. It's best for me to remain out of sight."

"Claire is not ashamed of you. I am not ashamed of you. Simon wants you. You must come." Elise, who rarely disagreed with her husband, had been adamant, and so he had joined his family in the coach.

The earl's widow, who was riding in the second coach with Charlie, had refused to lift a finger to arrange the funeral reception. This was not because she was overcome by grief; the fact is, she was furious. "I will never forgive him for this," she said as she stood with Claire and Simon watching as the earl's coffin was carried to the black draped hearse. "To grab a gun and go out to shoot a poacher by himself! It was just like him, though. He always thought he could do anything he wanted to. Stupid man."

Simon and Claire exchanged a look at the dowager's comment, and Simon's mouth twitched. Claire had to look away so she wouldn't giggle.

The dowager rounded on Simon. "I am not going to live in the Dower House," she announced, her pale eyes narrow with temper. "I am too young to shut myself away from life in the country. I want to live in the London house."

"We can certainly discuss that," Simon said in his mildest manner.

Claire thought she could see the smoke rising from the dowager's head, she was so angry. "I would kill him for this if he wasn't already dead," she said.

Simon's mouth twitched again, and Claire coughed into her hand. They were as pleased by the earl's death as his wife was furious, but, unlike the dowager, they were trying to maintain a decorous manner.

The funeral service was impressive, with the president and vice president of the Jockey Club giving ardent eulogies about Welbourne's contribution to English racing. When all of the mourners had filed out of the church, their coaches wended their way back to the abbey for the funeral reception Elise had organized.

This last week Claire had been hugely grateful for her mother. Elise may have been only fifteen when she fled France for Ireland, but she had been reared to be the wife of a great noble, and she knew how to deal with a large house filled with servants. It didn't take long for her to enlist Carstairs and Mrs. Willis as her loyal deputies. Like Claire, they were extremely relieved to discover that someone in the family knew how things should be done.

The house was draped in black when the carriages returned from the service, and the window drapes were drawn. There was more food than Claire had ever seen in her life, and footmen walked through the crowd with trays of wine. Claire thought that Simon was magnificent. Grave and beautiful, he stood beside Claire accepting condolences from his father's friends and distant family members he had never known existed. Claire, who knew how overwhelmed he was feeling, did her best to support him. She called upon all she had learned from Charlotte's governess, stood straight as a lance, and replied to the condolences with the graciousness of a seasoned hostess.

*

Elise felt it was her duty to mingle with the guests. She understood perfectly how closed an aristocratic circle could be, and she wanted to establish Claire's credentials for admittance. Elise was still beautiful, had a delightful French accent, and was a member of what had been one of the most closed aristocracies in the world. She had been reared to charm, and she had enough sense to exert that charm on the women, not the men. Women were the ones who ruled Society.

Though she didn't tell him, Elise was worried that Liam would find himself isolated in this kind of company. With Claire and Simon receiving, and herself circulating, he was left on his own. So she kept an eye on him, and was both surprised and pleased to see that he appeared to be the most popular person in the place. Jockey Club members surrounded him from the time they arrived until the time their carriages pulled away down the drive, leaving the family tired but relieved that everything had gone well.

*

Simon and Claire went to bed early. They had not yet moved into the earl's bedroom suite. The widow had made no mention of moving out, and Claire assured Simon she was perfectly happy in one of the guest bedrooms. In fact, she liked it much better than she thought she would like the bedroom where Simon's father and his wife had slept.

Simon was in bed first and Claire joined him, snuggling her head into his shoulder. His arm closed around her. He said, "Just think, one month ago you and I thought we might have to wait three years to be married."

"I know. She turned her head to kiss his jaw. "I always knew we were meant to be together."

"Do you know, I never really thought I would be the earl? I knew I was the heir, of course, but I just never believed it would happen."

"Did you think your horrible father was immortal?"

He laughed. "Perhaps I did."

"I wish I could give that poacher a reward," Claire said.

"He did get away."

"Good."

"Thank God my stepmother doesn't want to live in the Dower House. It's only half a mile away from here!"

"Will you let her live in the London house?"

"I'll let her live anywhere except near us."

"Amen," she said fervently.

He let out a long breath. "I had a long talk with Uncle Richard after you went to bed last night. He's going to help me. He said not to worry about money, he would make certain Welbourne was in good financial shape."

"I pray for Uncle Richard all the time," she said. "If it wasn't for him, and the trust fund, we wouldn't have been able to marry."

"I would have found some way," he said fiercely.

She arched her neck to smile up at him.

"Are you too tired?" he asked softly.

She knew that look in his eyes. "I am never too tired for you," she said turning toward him.

"I love you so much, Claire. I'll never get tired of saying how much I love you."

"And I'll never get tired of hearing it."

He gave a little groan and lowered his mouth to hers.

# CHAPTER TWENTY-THREE

*One Year Later*

The huge front lawn of Welbourne Abbey was crowded with a throng of men, women and boisterous children, all of them socializing around four large blue and white striped tents. Targets for archery had been set up in a corner of the lawn near a plantation of elms, and two cricket fields were laid out on the south lawn. The great Welbourne coach, drawn by four magnificent bay horses, was offering rides around the estate, and several farm wagons were transporting eager parents and children to the artificial lake, where boats were available. An orchestra set up in front of the abbey was playing lively music to accompany the festivities.

The Earl and Countess of Welbourne had invited their tenants and their friends from the neighborhood to celebrate the birth of their first son. The day was sunny and beautiful, and a radiant countess carried her month-old baby from group to group, showing him off. A number of the tenants commented among themselves that the young earl looked scarcely less radiant than his wife. To finish the picture, an exuberant Charlie hung off of Simon's hand, calling greetings to the tenant children he knew.

"God bless them all," Mrs. Thornton said to her husband, as they watched the procession of earl, countess, baby and Charlie around the grounds. "What a blessing it is that the old earl got shot."

Mr. Thomas looked around quickly, then spoke in a carefully lowered voice. "That might be true, Betsy, but it don't do to say it out loud like that."

"Nonsense," his wife returned forthrightly. "There's no a tenant farmer here who wouldn't agree. The young earl actually *cares* about us. He's fixed all the houses and he even built the Masons a new barn when theirs collapsed."

Farmer Thornton gazed fondly toward the young couple as they made their way back toward the house. "'Tis true, 'tis true.

139

He's a fine young man, the new earl. And his wife is verra kind." He grinned at his wife and said, "And verra pretty too."

She patted his arm and laughed.

\*

Claire was delighted that the baby had behaved so beautifully, smiling and cooing at his admiring audiences. When at last he started to fuss she said to Simon, "I'm going to take William back to the house and feed him. He's had enough company for today."

"He's been a trooper," his proud father said. "Charlie and I will continue to circulate."

"I'll come back after William is asleep."

"You don't have to come back, Claire." A faint frown puckered the skin between his eyebrows. "You must be tired."

Claire shifted the baby from one shoulder to the other. "Simon, I had a baby, not an accident. I'm perfectly fine. I'll come back."

"At least let me carry him upstairs for you."

"No. Stay here. I will be fine."

There was a pause, then he said, "I'm annoying you, aren't I?"

"Yes, you are. Look, here are Mr. and Mrs. Smithfield coming to talk to you." She turned away, saying over her shoulder, "I'll see you later."

Charlotte joined Claire at the abbey's front door. "May I come with you? Bruce Hendricks is pursuing me, and I can't stand him. But he's Geoffrey's friend and I mustn't be rude."

Claire smiled. "Come along. We can talk while I feed William."

"Thank you," Charlotte said feelingly, and Claire chuckled.

\*

Out on the lawn, and on the lake, the picnic continued. At four o'clock a lavish tea was served in the tents, with lemonade and ices for the children. At six o'clock the farmers began to leave for home to milk their cows, and the upper classes followed shortly afterward. The house servants had been busy all day, and Claire had given orders to a grateful staff that the family would require only a light supper that evening.

The immediate family, who had all helped with the picnic, gathered in the small drawing room after supper, a little tired, a little sunburned, but satisfied that the day had been a success.

Claire had excused everyone from dressing for dinner, but that was the only difference between the usual nightly gathering in the small sitting room and tonight. Claire was in her favorite place on the striped silk sofa, and Simon sat in his usual place beside her.

As she sipped her hot tea slowly, looking at the familiar, beloved faces around her, she thought of Charlie, safely tucked upstairs with his nanny. He had had such a good time today, running around with a group of little boys his age. Simon had been given custody of Charlie because he was the boy's closest male relative, but he allowed Charlie to visit his mother whenever the dowager wanted him. Of late, his visits were becoming fewer and shorter, which suited Charlie just fine.

The rest of the family were chatting comfortably, Liam and Elise sitting on the sofa opposite Claire's, and Uncle Richard in one of the large wingchairs facing the fire. Liam and Elise had moved into the abbey with Claire and Simon shortly after the earl's funeral. It was to have been a temporary arrangement, so Elise could help Claire with the new duties that had fallen upon her young shoulders. But it had worked out so well that Claire and Simon had begged them to stay. Elise, who understood how much her daughter relied on her, had convinced Liam to accept.

Richard Jarvis, though he didn't live at the abbey, was a most welcome member of their little family. He had been an enormous help to Simon. Jarvis had paid off the earl's gaming debts himself, and he had allowed Simon to access the trust fund money to make long overdue repairs to estate property. Simon, Jarvis, and Halleck, the estate agent, had worked out a financial plan for the future that would allow Welbourne to be both responsible and solvent. The first year of Simon's tenure had been busy and difficult, but rewarding.

*

Claire listened to the conversation going on around her and tried not to yawn. She was tired, but determined not to let Simon know. He did know, of course—he could read her like a book—but she wasn't going to admit it.

She had had a long, hard labor, and Simon had been terrified he was going to lose her. Elise had been with her the whole time, assuring her that everything was normal, that first babies were often long in coming, and Claire had soldiered through with clenched teeth, refusing to scream because she knew Simon would hear her. She had almost recovered her strength, but the strain of being gracious to so many people all at once had fatigued her. She knew all their tenants, knew their children and the names of their dogs, but facing them all together at the same time had been tiring.

She was stifling another yawn when something Jarvis was saying penetrated the fogginess of her brain.

"I'm going to Ireland in two weeks, Simon," she heard. "I want to visit Annabelle's grave. It's something I've always meant to do, and I've put it off for far too long. I wondered if you might care to come with me."

Claire felt Simon's relaxed body come to attention. "Yes," he said, and she could hear the eagerness in his voice. "I would like to come. I would like that very much."

Jarvis smiled with pleasure. "I hoped you'd say that. I think Annabelle would like it if the two of us came to visit her together."

As they began to discuss travel plans, Claire went rigid. She didn't want Simon to go to Ireland. In fact, everything in her was screaming against it. She had to keep him home. But, how? It was a perfectly reasonable thing for him to want to do. She listened to the thudding of her heart and knew she had to think of something.

Later, as she lay beside Simon in the great bed in the earl's room, she listened as he talked enthusiastically about the prospective trip. He ended by saying wistfully, "I wish I remembered my mother better. If she had lived, perhaps things would have been different between my father and me."

Claire doubted that, but remained silent. She had been wracking her brain, but hadn't yet come up with sufficient reason to keep Simon at home. Her da had called this feeling she had *"the sight,"* and told her she got it from his mother. She had felt it only twice before, once when her mother was planning to go visit an elderly woman from the parish, and once when Liam had been planning to bring Simon home from school. The first time she had succeeded in distracting her mother from the visit by pretending to be sick herself. The next day they had learned that a lantern had tipped over in the old woman's house and it had burned to the ground with the old woman in it. The second time she had convinced a skeptical Liam to check the chaise he was going to drive, and he had found one of the supports was dangerously cracked. That was when he told her about *the sight.*

And now she had the same feeling that something bad was going to happen to Simon if he went to Ireland. Everything in her wanted to beg him not to go, to stay home with her. He would probably give in when he saw how upset she was. But how selfish she would appear if she tried to keep him from visiting his mother's grave! Then she had an idea.

I'll get Da to go with him. If something should happen, Da will know what to do.

Simon was leaning over her and she lifted her mouth for his kiss. They had not made love in months, because of the baby, and she knew he was looking forward to her next visit to the doctor and hoping she would get his approval to resume their normal relationship.

His mouth lingered on hers and, for the first time since the baby, Claire felt desire stirring in her body.

"I'll put Uncle Richard off until after your doctor's visit," Simon said huskily. "That way I can say goodbye to you properly."

"Don't say goodbye," she said sharply. "Never say that to me, Simon."

He gave her a puzzled look. "All right, I won't say it then. What would you like me to say?"

"Just tell me you love me." She could hear the quiver in her voice.

"Are you all right, Claire?"

She got a grip on herself and managed a smile. "I'm perfectly fine—just rather tired."

"Then go to sleep, my love. You'll feel better tomorrow."

She nodded, he kissed her again and they settled themselves to sleep.

# CHAPTER TWENTY-FOUR

The following morning Claire sought her father at the stud farm. Liam was in his office doing paperwork, and she closed the door for privacy. As he looked up from his desk, she said urgently, "I need to talk to you, Da."

He pushed his desk chair back and gestured Claire to the chair opposite him. "What is it, girl? You look worried."

She sat and looked into her father's eyes, the eyes that were so like her own. "I want you to go to Ireland with Simon," she said. "I'd go if I could, but since I can't, I want you to go in my place."

His forehead creased and his eyes narrowed. "Claire, why in the world should I go to Ireland with Simon?"

Claire said, "I'm nursing a new baby, Da. I can't go and I need you to go in my stead. Simon can't be allowed to go alone!"

Liam lifted expressive black eyebrows. "Simon won't be alone; he's travelling with Richard Jarvis. Jarvis is a rich and powerful man, and Simon is an English earl. Nothing is going to happen to either of them, especially in Limerick. The United Irishmen have been fairly crushed in that area."

She leaned forward, willing him to understand. "It's just...Da I have the feeling. The way I did when I told you there was something wrong with your carriage. Remember, you told me I had *the sight*, that I had inherited it from your mother?"

"I remember," Liam said quietly. He regarded her in silence for a long moment. Then, "What are you afraid of?"

She made a restless movement with her hands. "I don't know! I just have this feeling that something bad is going to happen to Simon and one of us needs to be with him."

Liam regarded her gravely. There was gray at his temples now, and the squint lines at the corners of his eyes were deeper. He had just turned fifty, and he looked and acted like a man accustomed to authority. When he remained silent, Claire slid toward the front of her chair and said pleadingly, "Next to me and William, Simon loves you best of anyone in the world. You know that. He even named his first son after you!"

Liam smiled. "And you know Simon is like a son to me. But I really don't think he will be in any danger, Claire. They're not touring the country; they're going to visit a grave, and then they're coming home. If I thought there was real danger I wouldn't want him to go at all."

"Da, please," she held her clasped hands to her breast as she made her plea.

"I have too much work to do here, Claire; I don't want to miss the time. You know that Simon and I want to get the costs of the stud under control. Lord Welbourne bought too many mares, and we've had too many foals that didn't turn out to be racers. I know I can make the stud profitable again, and I have some buyers coming next week to look at two of the mares..." He stopped abruptly as Claire stood up.

"That's all right, Da. I understand. I'll just go myself and take William with me."

Liam stood as well. "Absolutely not." They looked at each other, then he sighed with resignation, "If you feel as strongly as that *beag amhain,* then I will go to Ireland with Simon."

"*Thank you,* Da." She came around the desk and hugged him. "I'll feel much more comfortable if you are with him."

He patted her back. "Do not be worrying yourself over Simon. I'll take good care of him, I promise you."

She looked up to him, a smile on her lips, tears in her eyes. "I know you will, Da. You always have."

*

Liam told Simon he would like to see Ireland again and asked if he could join Simon and his uncle on their trip. Simon, who was always happy to spend time with his father-in-law, gladly agreed. Nor did he seem to find anything strange in Liam's request, which was a relief to Claire.

The night before he left, Simon and Claire made love for the first time since the baby. Afterward he held her in his arms while she slept, breathing in the scent of her hair and skin. He didn't want to leave her, but he had so much, and his mother had had so little. It felt right that he should make this pilgrimage to her grave.

He had so much. Sometimes, when he was sitting with the family after dinner, he would look around and think: We've done it. We're married. We have a baby. We have Liam and Elise and Uncle Richard, who will always love us and help us. We have this beautiful home to pass down to our son. And William will grow up knowing his father loves him.

As he lay awake in the dark room, his sleeping wife in his arms, Simon rested his lips on her hair, his heart so full of love he thought it might burst out of his chest. All of this was because of Claire, he thought. Everything good in his life was because of her.

"Thank you," he whispered into the soft hair under his mouth. "Thank you, Claire, for loving me." Then, carefully, he slid away from her into his own part of the bed and closed his eyes to sleep.

# CHAPTER TWENTY-FIVE

Simon rapped on the door of the early Georgian stone house that went by the name of Castle Asenath. The three men waited for a full two minutes before an elderly man with a shock of gray hair answered the door.

"Ah!" he said in surprise, thick gray eyebrows lifted in amazement.

Simon produced a pleasant smile. "You must be Donovan. I did send you a notice that I would be arriving with two guests. I am the new Lord Welbourne."

The day was dark and overcast and all of a sudden the heavens opened. "For God's sake, man," Richard Jarvis said. "Step away from the door and let us in."

The entry hall the three men stepped into was unlighted and furnished with a single table and chair. Simon looked around and mentally shivered. *What a dreary looking place*, he thought.

The butler finally spoke. "We received your letter, my lord, and we are prepared to receive you." The words sounded as if they had been memorized. Then he added, as a palpable after-thought, "I'm sorry about your da."

"Thank you," Simon said. "Our baggage is in the carriage out in front. Is there someone who can carry it in for us and see to the horses? The coachman will also need a place to sleep. He will be driving us back to the coast in a few days."

"I'll see to it, my lord. Now, if you gentlemen will come into the parlor, I'll get Timmy to bring in your bags and take the coachman to the stables. Mrs. Fitzsimmons, our housekeeper, will be down to ye soon."

Simon, Liam and Richard followed Donovan down a narrow hallway into a smallish room. Two sofas were placed in front of the fireless chimneypiece, above which hung a painting of a man on horseback surrounded by foxhounds. The other walls were decorated with a limited variety of hunting scenes.

The room was frigid.

"Might we have a fire here, Donovan?" Simon asked.

The butler looked harried. "I'll see what I can do, m'lord," he mumbled.

Richard Jarvis spoke in his most commanding voice, "Get the fire going. It's freezing in here."

Donovan gave him an injured look. "Young Sean is home today sick. His lordship never gave us an exact date as to when he would arrive."

Liam said something in Irish and Donovan's head snapped up. He replied in the same language, and hurried off.

"I think we'll get that fire," Liam said with grim satisfaction.

Simon said curiously, "What did you say to him, Liam?"

"I told him to move his lazy arse and get some wood for the fire."

Simon looked around the room in bewilderment. "This is not exactly what I had expected to find. Mr. Halleck never mentioned that the castle itself was a ruin and the family lived in a house that had been built on the property." He walked to one of the two windows in the room and stared through the dirty glass at the ancient three-story stone tower that stood some quarter-mile away.

"You can see towers like that all over the country." Liam spoke behind him with palpable bitterness. "Many of them were built during the time of Cromwell, when the English were busy devastating the whole of Ireland."

Simon noted that his father-in-law's Irish accent, which had faded somewhat during his years in England, had come back the minute he set foot on Irish soil. Simon turned from the window and asked, "Do you think we have a chance of getting dinner here?"

"God, I hope so," Jarvis said. "I'm starving."

"Oh, they'll be a cook," Liam said. "The servants have to eat, after all."

Jarvis said, "I don't like this, Simon. When you and I went over the books for this place they showed there was a cook, a scullery maid, a housemaid, a footman, a butler and five men to work on the property. Do you remember?"

"I do, Uncle Richard," Simon said. "That's why I didn't think they'd be any problem with us making this visit."

Liam said, "Who makes this report to your estate agent?"

"Halleck hired a solicitor from Limerick to oversee the household here and make twice yearly reports on income and expenditure."

"And the last time any member of the family visited here was when Simon's mother died. That was...fourteen or so years ago?"

"Yes," Simon said.

Jarvis said in an outraged voice, "And since then the Earl of Welbourne has been paying for all these servants who don't seem to exist!"

Simon looked at Liam and saw on his face what he had expected to see. He sighed and turned to his uncle. "This is what happens when an owner neglects his responsibilities and becomes an absentee landlord. My father—and I—are to blame for the situation here, not these people."

"Nonsense," Jarvis snapped. "That solicitor in Limerick is to blame. I'm sure he's being paid to lie to us."

"Of course he is," Simon said. "But we're here to visit my mother's grave, Uncle Richard. I don't want to worry about the servants' honesty right now."

Richard opened his mouth to protest and Liam cut in. "The boy is right. You need to hold your tongue, Jarvis, and let us do what we came to do. Wait until you get home and have time to think before you start roaring around here accusing people."

Jarvis turned to his nephew to protest, but Simon said, pleasantly but definitely, "We'll talk about it when we get home, Uncle Richard."

Jarvis looked surprised, then thoughtful. "Very well, Simon. If that's what you want."

"It is."

Donovan came back into the room accompanied by a boy carrying an armload of wood. "This is Timmy. He'll be making the fire for you."

Simon looked at the young man, who was dripping wet, and said mildly, "I thought you were taking our horses to the stable."

The clear blue eyes of Ireland looked serenely into Simon's. "I showed the coachman where to go and he said he'd take care o' the horses since I was after having to make the fire."

Simon, taking in that guileless blue gaze, had to fight down a grin. He was beginning to find this whole situation amusing.

"Thank you, Timmy," he said courteously.

Liam gave him a quick look, then the corner of Liam's lip twitched as well. The two looked away from each other before they started to laugh.

"This is disgraceful," Jarvis was muttering. "Disgraceful."

Liam said, "Have you a dram in the house?"

The butler perked up. "We do that. Would you gentlemen like a taste of good Irish whiskey?"

Simon and Liam's chorus of "Yes," clashed with Jarvis' protest.

Simon gave his uncle his most charming smile. "When in Rome..."

Jarvis grumbled.

Simon turned to the butler, "How long have you worked here, Donovan?"

"Some eight year, my lord."

Simon felt a stab of disappointment. He had been hoping one of the servants might have lived here at the time of his mother's death. He knew so little about it. He didn't even know where she was buried.

Liam was saying, "Is there anyone in the house who has lived here for longer than that?"

"Our housekeeper, Mrs. Fitzsimmons. She's been here for over twenty year. She'll be with you soon enough. I had to wake her from her nap." He glanced at Timmy, who was busy with the fire, then said, "I'll go and fetch that whiskey."

"Taking a nap?" Jarvis said in horror as the door closed behind Donovan.

"If she's been here for twenty years she's probably pretty old," Simon said, relieved to discover there was indeed someone here who had known his mother.

Timmy turned around. "She's old all right, but she's still sharp as a knife, my lord. She's a grand housekeeper. There's no need to replace her."

"Thank you for telling me," Simon said gravely.

The wet brown head nodded and the boy stood up. "Fire's ready. I'll go now and see if that coachman has done right by the horses."

"I appreciate that," Simon said, still speaking gravely.

The boy gave him a grin and went out the door. They heard him whistling as he went down the hall.

Liam started to laugh, and Jarvis growled, "This is a disgrace."

Donovan came in with a tray upon which reposed a bottle of whiskey and three glasses. He put it on the table that lay between the two sofas and the three men moved to take seats in front of the fire. The door opened again and a thin, white-haired woman in a black dress and black shawl came slowly into the room. She was leaning on a cane.

Simon jumped up from the sofa. "Mrs. Fitzsimmons?" he asked.

"I'm that sorry I wasn't here to greet you, my lord," she said in a soft Irish voice. "I hope that good-for-nothing Donovan made you welcome."

The old woman was coming toward him and Simon stepped forward to meet her. She smiled, looked up at him, and every ounce of color drained from her face. "Jesus, Mary and Joseph," she said making the sign of the cross. "Is it the truth you're telling me? Are you truly the new Earl of Welbourne?"

This kind of reaction had happened to him once before and Simon felt as if he had been punched in the gut. He struggled to catch his breath and then Liam had his arm and was saying, "Sit down, son. You're white as a sheet."

"...I'm all right," he said, although he knew he wasn't. "Better get the old woman before she falls."

"Jarvis has her. Come, sit down and have a dram. You're in shock."

Obediently Simon followed the older man's instructions. After the dram had gone down he felt stronger and looked at the woman who was now sitting on the sofa opposite him. She was sipping from the dram Jarvis was holding to her lips. As Simon watched, the color came slowly back to her face.

"I'm that sorry, my lord, for making such a fool of myself. But it was such a shock seeing you..."

Simon leaned forward and stared commandingly into her eyes. They were veined but not cloudy. "Whom do I remind you of, Mrs. Fitzsimmons?" he asked, making a great effort to speak gently.

When she just stared at him in distress, he said, "You're not the first person to say I look like someone else, and my face is not a common one." His voice hardened as he repeated, "Whom do I remind you of?"

The old lady looked pleadingly at Liam. He said something to her in Irish and she replied in the same language. He spoke again and she looked down at her old hands clasped tightly in her black cloth lap and nodded.

"What did you say?" Simon asked Liam.

"I told her to answer your question, that you wouldn't rest until you found out the truth."

"It's true," Simon said, looking at the woman. He asked once again, "Whom do I remind you of?"

Her old voice was unsteady as she answered, her eyes glued to her work worn hands, "There was a young English officer who used to visit here. It was over twenty year ago now. I wasn't the housekeeper then, I was one of the maids. But I never forgot his face—he was that beautiful."

Simon's heart was pounding so loudly he could hardly speak. "Do you remember his name?"

"I remember he was called Tom. He was a Lieutenant."

Simon turned to Liam. "Mr. Cookson's brother's name was Thomas, and he was an officer in Ireland when he died."

The housekeeper said softly, "It was thought he was shot by one of the United Irishmen. They were active around here twenty year ago."

Richard Jarvis said suddenly, "Was Lady Welbourne here when the lieutenant came to visit? Did he come here to see her?"

The wrinkles on the old woman's face seemed to deepen as she looked at Simon. "Yes, he came to see your mother, my lord." A tear trickled down her face and her voice shook. "I'm that sorry for what my foolishness has done."

"Don't be sorry," Simon said, and his voice was unrecognizable even to himself. "Just tell me what happened. I need to know. I need to know about...my father."

# CHAPTER TWENTY-SIX

Simon listened to the old woman's story as if his life hung on every word she uttered. The countess and the young lieutenant had become friendly, she said, and in the earl's absence had taken to riding out together whenever he could get free. "The poor boy was killed three days before the earl's return, and her ladyship was grieving hard." Her eyes met Simon's in an urgent look. "Believe me, my lord, no one in this household ever mentioned your mam's friendship with the English lieutenant. We liked her ladyship that much. She were a very sweet lady."

Somehow Simon managed to give her a reassuring smile.

She took a deep breath and went on, "But the earl must have heard gossip from somewhere, because within two days of his return he hurried her ladyship away. I still remember how white and frail she looked. We all felt that sorry for her. Nobody liked the earl. He was a right bastard, he was."

"Yes, he was." Simon said evenly. "So my fa...the earl...never actually saw Tom Clarkson?"

"He never did, my lord."

Liam turned to Simon, "So he could never be quite sure."

"He was sure, Liam." Listening to his mother's pitiful story, Simon thought it was a good thing the earl was dead because Simon would have murdered him if he were still alive.

Richard Jarvis, who had been stupefied by the housekeeper's story, said, "So, what all this means, Simon, is that James Radley wasn't your father? Your real father was this Lieutenant Cookson?"

Simon returned his uncle's stunned look and nodded slowly. "It seems pretty clear, doesn't it?"

The idea that he might not be the earl's son had never occurred to Simon. He thought of all those years spent wondering what it was he had done to make his father hate him so, and now he had the answer.

My poor mother, he thought with a rush of sympathy. How that bastard must have made her suffer.

He couldn't help but think of himself and Claire, how lucky they were to have what his mother had been denied. He said abruptly, "Perhaps that's why my mother came back here five years later. She wanted to revisit the place where she had been happy. Perhaps she even wanted to visit my father's grave."

The housekeeper had been silent for a while and now Jarvis asked her, "You must have been here at the castle when my sister returned, Mrs. Fitzsimmons. "Can you tell us about that visit? Can you tell us how she died? All we were told was she had pneumonia."

"I was here," she said reluctantly, and looked down at the hands clasped in her lap.

Simon leaned toward her. "That's what my nanny told me. She said that my father had received a letter saying my mother died of pneumonia and had been buried in Ireland. That's all I've ever known."

Mrs. Fitzsimmons' head lifted in surprise. "But the earl was here with her," she said.

Stunned silence filled the room. Finally Jarvis spoke, "My family was told she had rashly decided to go to Ireland while the earl was visiting friends in Devon. Supposedly he heard the news of her death when he returned to Welbourne."

The old lady looked from Simon to Jarvis, then back again to Simon. What she saw made her sit up straight, and her face set with resolution. "The earl was here, my lord," she said. "They came together."

Simon had a sick feeling deep in his stomach. "Mrs. Fitzgerald, I need to know what happened here," he said. "I need to know what happened to my mother."

*

Liam knocked softly on the door to Simon's bedroom. The boy had been white and silent during the surprisingly decent dinner the cook had prepared. Liam and Richard Jarvis had done their best to keep some conversation going, but as soon as the pudding was served Simon had excused himself and gone to his room.

Silence was the only answer to Liam's knock.

Claire had been right, Liam thought. Something shocking had happened to Simon during this visit, and Liam was very glad he was here. Jarvis cared about the boy, of course, but he didn't know him the way Liam did.

He knocked again and called softly, "Simon, it's Liam. Open the door, son. I'm worried about you."

There was no sound from inside but suddenly the door opened. "Come in," Simon said.

There was a chair pulled up to the room's single window. Simon gestured toward it and smiled crookedly. "I was just looking out at the rain."

Liam went to the chair and moved it to the fireplace, where a fire was actually burning. "Sit," he said, and sat himself on a settee facing the chair.

Slowly Simon came to join him. His eyes on the wood-burning fire, he said in a constricted voice, "Mrs. Fitzsimmons thinks he killed her. She wouldn't say so precisely, but it was clear as day. They went for a walk by the river and my mother fell in and drowned. How likely does that sound to you?"

"Not likely at all," Liam returned grimly. "After you went upstairs I asked her if there had been an inquiry, but of course there hadn't. After all, who was there to make an official inquiry against the Earl of Welbourne? The servants, who suspected what had happened? The Irish court system? There isn't any Irish court system, only an English one. How likely was it that the English would inquire even if they did suspect foul play?"

"They wouldn't."

"Of course they wouldn't. And here in England no one knew he had been in Ireland with her. The Jarvises, who certainly would

159

have called for an inquiry if they knew the truth, all thought the earl was in England when his wife died."

Silence fell as the two of them stared into the flickering fire. Then Liam said, "What I don't understand is why, after *five years*, he would feel it necessary to kill her. He was taking a chance, after all. Someone could have seen him."

Simon was white and dark shadows had appeared under his eyes. He said, "I can answer that question. He had gone through all my mother's money and he needed to marry another heiress to get more. Which is precisely what he did. My stepmother had a very substantial dowry—which he also went through, I might add."

Liam's heart ached for him. What could he say that would be a help? He sighed and came out with the best he could do. "Well, boyo, take comfort from the thought that he is roasting in hell right this very minute, while your mother is an angel in heaven along with her Tom."

Simon got up and went to sit next to his father-in-law on the settee. Liam put an arm around the boy's shoulders and hugged him.

After a moment of silence, Simon asked, "What do you think my mother would have done if Tom had lived?"

Liam sighed. "I don't know, Simon. They were together for so short a time—a month, the old lady said—while your...the earl...was hunting with friends up in Roscommon. And their situation was impossible, really. She was the wife of a powerful earl and he was a mere lieutenant. I don't see what they could have done."

"Well, I'm glad that man is not my real father. I'm glad I don't carry a single particle of his rotten blood in my body!"

"He sounds as if he was a grand lad, Tom Cookson." Liam paused. "Even if he was an English soldier."

That brought a flicker of a smile to Simon's face.

Liam said, "You must have been a great joy to her, Simon. Every time she looked at you, she would know that a part of him lived on, that she had been able to give him that."

Simon pressed his lips together and nodded. When he was able to speak again, he said, "Charlie should be the Earl of Welbourne, not me. Do you know what I need to do to turn it over to him?"

The question surprised Liam and it was a moment before he could answer. "You can't turn it over, son. If it were possible to do such a thing, don't you think the earl would have done it himself? You know he hated the thought of you succeeding him, but he never tried to disinherit you. You were his legitimate son, born in a legal marriage. Naming you a bastard would have caused a scandal, for sure, but it wouldn't have changed things."

"But it's not fair," Simon protested. "It's Charlie's by right of blood."

"Simon. I'm certain you're not the first cuckoo to step into the shoes of his supposed father. The aristocracy is not exactly famous for faithfulness to the marriage vow."

"But I have to *try*, Liam. I feel like a thief who's stolen something from his own brother!"

"Think, son. Do you really want to stand up in public and tell the world your mother was an adulteress?"

Simon turned, staring at his father-in-law in shock. "Is that what you think of her?"

"Of course not! I think of her as a lovely young girl who was married to a devil. She fell in love with a fine young man, who loved her back. I think she was tragic, Simon, and I would hate to see her the subject of disgusting gossip."

"I could never do that to her!" Simon's eyes were bright with emotion.

"Then do your best for Charlie as his big brother. Let him know you love him and will always be there for him."

"The way you always did for me," Simon said.

Liam smiled. "Yes, the way I did for you."

"I want to see Tom's grave too."

"So do I, son. We'll go tomorrow morning to your mother's and then drive into Limerick city and pay our respects to your father."

*

The following day was as lovely as the previous day had been miserable. The three men drove in their hired coach to the small church on the River Shannon where the housekeeper had told them Annabelle Jarvis Radley was buried. Richard Jarvis put his arm around Simon's shoulder as they stood looking at the granite stone with her name and the dates of her birth and death chiseled into the stark stone. "She was such a beautiful, loving girl," he said in a choking voice.

"I wish I had known her better," Simon whispered.

Richard's arm tightened. "She knew you, lad. She had you for five years, and I know you were the joy of her life."

Simon felt tears sting his eyes; two drops slid onto his cheeks and rolled downward. He ignored them. "I hope so," he said.

Lieutenant Tom Cookson was buried in the cemetery attached to St. John's Castle, the English bastion on the River Shannon in Limerick city. His marker was small and had been hard to find.

As Simon stood looking at his father's name and dates, he was swept by such a wave of sorrow it threatened to engulf him. These young parents of his...what a tragic end their love had come to... And he had been so lucky. It wasn't fair.

Liam spoke next to his ear, "The two of them are looking down on you from heaven, my boy, and they're very proud. Never doubt that."

Simon turned to his father-in-law. "I hope that's true."

"It is, son. It is," Liam said with certitude.

Suddenly all Simon wanted was to see Claire. The revelation of the last two days had torn him apart, and only she could heal the

162

wounds. Only she could give him the peace of mind he so desperately needed.

"I want to go home," he said, and even to his own ears he sounded like a child.

"We'll leave tomorrow," Liam said.

"That's fine with me," Jarvis agreed.

Simon closed his eyes, wishing an angel could fly him home to Claire *now*. He took a deep breath, gathered himself together, opened his eyes, attempted a smile, and said, "Good."

# EPILOGUE

*Ten Years Later*

It had been raining all week, but the day of Welbourne's annual lawn party for tenants and friends dawned sunny and warm. "Thank heavens," Claire said to Simon over the breakfast table. "We've always been fortunate with the weather. I don't know where we would have put all those people if it continued to rain."

"You could have postponed it," Liam said, looking up from his plate of eggs and kippers.

"No, I'm afraid we couldn't," Elise said in her gentle voice. "All the food has been bought and it would go bad if we canceled."

Simon said, "Well, the sun is shining and the grass should be dry by this afternoon, so there's nothing to worry about." He smiled at Claire. "You won't have to have all those muddy feet tramping around your house."

"Thank heaven," she returned seriously. "The poor maids would have been scrubbing floors for a week!"

Liam patted his mouth with his napkin. "If you will excuse me, I promised to take the boys down to the stables to help braid the ponies' manes and tails."

In previous years the pony rides had proved to be a huge success with their younger guests. This year was the first time nine-year-old William and seven-year-old Richard were being allowed to lead their ponies around the paddock that had been set aside for the event. They were both very puffed up at being given such an important task.

Charlie said, "I suppose I'm in charge of the boats again?"

Simon looked at his younger brother, who had arrived at Welbourne only yesterday. "You're the one who knows how to swim. Just keep in mind last year, when you let too many get in a boat and one of them fell out. You don't want to have to dive into the lake to rescue someone again, Charlie."

165

"Don't worry Simon," Charlie replied with a grin. "That was not an experience I want to repeat."

"No more than four, Charlie," Simon said.

"No more than four," Charlie returned solemnly, as he made his way to the breakfast table to refill his plate.

Simon looked at his brother's long, slim back and reflected once again how fortunate it was that Charlie had been allowed to grow up at Welbourne. His mother had married a marquis two years after her first husband's death, and he had never been keen on sharing his wife with "another man's brat." So Charlie had lived with Simon and Claire, taking lessons with a tutor until he was thirteen and had to go away to school.

He was starting Oxford in the autumn. Unlike his older brother, he was eager to attend university. Charlie had proved to be an outstanding student, and Richard Jarvis had promised him an excellent position in the bank when he graduated. Charlie had no aristocratic qualms about becoming a banker. "I can make a lot of money working for Uncle Richard, and I'll get to use my brain as well," he had told Simon and Claire when they discussed the offer with him. "That's far better than lolling around London, gambling and going to dances. What a bore!"

When Simon thought of what might have happened if Charlie had turned out to be like his father, he shuddered. If it hadn't been for Uncle Richard, Welbourne would have sunk under the weight of the earl's debts. Simon always felt it was a small miracle that Charlie was so unlike either of his parents.

Simon pushed his chair back now and stood. "I'm going to walk around the grounds to make certain everything is in proper train for this afternoon."

Claire stood as well. "I'll go with you."

"Good. Are you ready to go now or shall I wait for you?"

"I'm ready," she replied, coming around the table to join him.

"The grass will still be wet," he warned, looking at her shoes.

"Pooh," she returned, and he grinned.

*

As the two of them stepped out into the sunshine, Claire looked up at her husband and smiled. His perfect profile was calm, but she could feel the enthusiasm that was bubbling inside him. He loved this day. He loved seeing all the people who belonged to Welbourne happy, well fed, and enjoying themselves. He loved entertaining his friends. Charlie had told him once that he was becoming quite a *paterfamilias*. When Claire had asked what that meant, Charlie had grinned and said, "The father of a Roman family. Only in Simon's case, the family includes every living creature on the estate."

It was true, Claire thought, as she walked beside Simon in the brilliant sunshine. There wasn't an adult, child, horse or dog that lived on Welbourne property that Simon didn't know well. The farms were all in pristine condition, and the income Welbourne's owner received from them was more than sufficient to sustain his own expenses. Simon went up to London occasionally, when there was a vote in Parliament that interested him, and Claire had been presented at court, but most of the time they lived at Welbourne. They weren't rich, but they were very comfortable.

Claire's shoes were getting wet from the grass, but she ignored them. Simon took her hand and said, "I've been thinking the weather isn't the only thing we've been lucky with," he said.

She leaned her head briefly against his shoulder. "I know. I'm so happy that sometimes it scares me."

He stopped and turned to her. "You've had your sorrows too, Claire," he said in his softest voice.

She knew what he meant. A year ago she had miscarried of a little girl, and she had worried everyone by her profound grief.

She looked up at the sky and said quietly, "I know. But I've given her up to God now, Simon. I know she's safe with Him."

He lifted her hand to his lips, and, as his lips touched her palm, she looked up into his beloved face. He was older now, and that morning of the world beauty of his youth had matured. His hair was as fair, and his eyes the same crystalline blue, but the marks of confidence and authority were stamped on his features. Over the last ten years he had grown into his position as Earl of Welbourne, and now it was ingrained in him to the point where he never even thought about it.

She forgot about the people who might be watching, decided not to wait any longer, and stood on tiptoe to say into his ear, "We're going to have a baby."

She knew how much he loved being a father, so she wasn't surprised when a huge smile blazed across his face. His arms closed around her and held her tightly. His mouth was pressed to the top of her head so his words were muffled when he spoke. "I'm so glad, Claire. I know how you grieved for the baby you lost. I'm so glad you'll have another one to hold in your arms."

"I am too," she said. "But I won't call her Charlotte. Charlotte was the name...." Suddenly she couldn't go on and he held her even tighter."

"Charlotte will understand, Claire. She has two babies of her own. She'll understand."

"I know she will."

"Good God," Simon said, and Claire felt his arms loosen. "We seem to have become the center of interest."

Claire looked toward the tents and saw her servants hastily turning away and getting back to work.

They stepped apart and as they did a little boy ran up to them, followed by a younger one. The older one, who had inherited his father's hair and eyes, said breathlessly, "Mama, Grandpapa wants to know what color yarn we should use to braid the ponies."

"Red, I think, William," Claire said.

The second boy, who had his mother's coloring, arrived. "Hello Mama, Hello Papa," he said with a beaming smile. "We're going to braid the ponies. Grandpapa is going to show us how."

"So I heard," Claire said.

Simon said, "I want you boys to remember that the children who will be riding have probably never sat on a horse in their lives. You are to *walk* with them. Do Not Trot The Ponies. Is that clear?"

"But what if some of them do know how to ride?" Richard asked. "It will be boring for them to just walk around."

"Then they can be bored." Simon's voice was final.

"Yes, Papa," they chorused.

Claire smothered a smile as the boys ran off.

"We don't need any broken bones today," Simon muttered.

"They'll be all right," Claire said. "The boys won't disobey you, Simon. Besides, Sid will be watching them."

"Mmmm," he said, not sounding entirely convinced.

"I should get back to the house," Claire said. "Charlotte is coming over early in case I need some help."

"If the weather holds we can ride tomorrow morning," he said.

Claire smiled. They had been stuck in all week with the foul weather. "Let's hope."

He turned around with her. "Liam has a new horse for me to work with. He's a stunning-looking black."

"Will he jump?"

"I think so. Orion is getting too old to take out hunting and if this one's as good as Liam thinks, perhaps I'll keep him."

"Tell me about him," she said eagerly, and he began to talk as they walked toward the splendid stone front of Welbourne Abbey.

# Acknowledgment

I would like to express my heartfelt thanks to Susie Felber, the daughter of my dear friend, Edith Felber, who wrote regencies under the name of Edith Layton. I miss Edith terribly, but having Susie has been a great blessing. She makes me feel that Edith isn't that far away—she is very like her mom. And when I was completely baffled about how to get hooked up with social media, Susie came to my rescue.

The reason I have a lovely website; the reason I have an attractive newsletter; the reason I have any means at all of contacting my readers—the reason is Susie. She set everything up for me, told me how to use it, got out my monthly newsletter, and answered all my idiotic questions. She has her mother's generous and compassionate heart and I want to thank her for everything she has done for me.

# About the Author

Joan Wolf is a *USA TODAY* bestselling author whose highly reviewed books include some forty novels set in the period of the English Regency. She fell in love with the Regency when she was a young girl and discovered the novels of Georgette Heyer. Although she has strayed from the period now and then, it has always remained her favorite.

Joan was born and brought up in New York City but has spent most of her adult life with her husband and two children in Connecticut. She has a passion for animals and over the years has filled the house with a variety of much-loved dogs and cats. Her great love for her horses has spilled over into every book she has written. The total number of her published novels is fifty-three and she has no plans to retire.

*"Joan Wolf never fails to deliver the best."*
—Nora Roberts

*"Joan Wolf is absolutely wonderful. I've loved her work for years."*
—Iris Johansen

*"As a writer, she's an absolute treasure."*
—Linda Howard

*"Strong, compelling fiction."*
—Amanda Quick

*"Joan Wolf writes with an absolute emotional mastery that goes straight to the heart."*
—Mary Jo Putney

*"Wolf's Regency historicals are as delicious and addictive as dark, rich, Belgian chocolates."*
—Publishers Weekly

*"Joan Wolf is back in the Regency saddle—hallelujah!"*
—Catherine Coulter

\* \* \*

*To sign up for Joan's newsletter, email her at joanemwolf@gmail.com.*

CPSIA information can be obtained
at www.ICGtesting.com
Printed in the USA
FSHW021142080720
71488FS